On My Own

Kesha K. Redmon

Kandour Publishing

Kandour Publishing
P.O. Box 18300
Memphis, TN 38181-0300

Manufactured in the United States of America

ISBN: 0-9791225-0-3
ISBN: 978-0-9791225-0-7

Dedication

This book is dedicated to all the women making it
on their own. Keep your head up.

Do your best to present yourself to God as
one approved, a workman who does not need
to be ashamed and who correctly handles
the word of truth.

2 Timothy 2-15

Debra
God Bless
Ktre d
6/2/07

Acknowledgements

First of all, I would like to thank Him who holds my hand. If it had not been for You on my side, I truly don't know where I would be.

I would like to thank my family. My grandmother, Vinellar, who after raising nine of her own decided to take in four more. To my aunts Sue, B.J., Mary Francis, Annie Rose, Audrey Mae, Uncle Charles, thanks for putting your lives on hold to make sure that ours would be well lived.

To my sister Carolyn, brother Gary, and my cousin—who is truly a sister in every way that matters, Angela "D.D." Redmon.

To Shondrika, Latrischa, Janecia, Edward, Catreal and My'elle, always do your best in what ever you do. Somebody will always be watching.

To Dionne Jones thanks for listening and encouraging.

To my girl, Aretha J. "The Scholar" Lee, I can't imagine not having you as a friend, besides who could I possibly tell all my secrets to. I'm so glad that we attended the same college. I don't know if there is another person out there I could spend hours upon hours talking with on the phone. Anyway, May the Lord watch between me and thee while we're absent one from another until we meet again. Dang. Is that you calling already? I'm so proud of you.

Lastly, to my editor, Chandra Sparks Taylor, thank you so much for your patience and understanding in helping me see what this project could really be.

To all my sisters doing you, keep the faith.

Love, Kesha K. Redmon

What's a Girl to Do?

Once again, it's twelve-thirty, and there is no sign of Tori. It must be wonderful not having to work. I guess being married to a sports agent does have its advantages. Natori Lang and I have been friends for what seems like forever. We actually met three years ago at Baskin Robbins, here in Atlanta, Georgia. She was six months pregnant with her daughter, Nylondria, whom we call Nyla. I was in low-self mode, trying to drown my woes in a dark chocolate double cone. We ended up having a long conversation, and we've been friends ever since. Her friendship couldn't have come at a better time. I was feeling alone in the world. My parents died when I was twelve, leaving my grandmother to take care of me. After I lost her six years ago, my life hasn't been the same. The way I learned to deal with my loneliness is to drown myself in my work.

Tori really hasn't had to work hard, coming from a prestigious family and all. Her father is an attorney, and her mother is a retired professor. Now she gets to keep living the life of champagne wishes and caviar dreams. It's good though because Andre cherishes her and loves the ground his daughter walks on.

Romy's has been Tori and my destination for lunch for months. The restaurant has the best pasta I have ever tasted. It's also a bonus because it's only two blocks away from my job at the Alpha Science Institute. Just when I am about to call it a day, in walks Tori dressed head to toe in Donna Karan with black leather Monolo Blahniks to boot.

"Hey, girl. What's up? I'm sorry I'm late. Nyla's nanny was late again. I think I'm going to have to fire her."

"Tori, you know Sarella has a family of her own. You should allow her time to spend with her own kids. And plus, you could have easily brought Nyla with you."

"Kaye, the last thing I need is to be bothered with a wailing two-year- old with attachment issues."

"That's something for you to say about your own daughter."

"Chile, please. She is strictly a daddy's little girl. Dre gives her entirely too much."

"Umph. Sounds familiar. Just like her mother."

"Don't start, bitch."

"Why must you always refer to me in such vile, derogatory terms?"

"Because I love you, girl."

"Whatever."

"Anyway, what are you having for lunch?"

"I think I'm going to order the usual, chicken parmesan with pasta."

Tori orders the grilled chicken with fettuccine alfredo.

After the waiter leaves, I look up at Tori, and she's definitely up to something. I can actually see the wheels of thought turning in her head.

"What are you up to?"

"Oh, I was just thinking. When was the last time you had a vacation?" she asks.

"Tori, I was just off a week ago."

"No, no. I'm talking about a real vacation. You were off then because you had to attend a medicinal chemistry conference. That sounds nothing like a vacation. I'm referring to the one where you remove your body physically from its current status to relax not work."

"I have a job. I'm a chemist. I can't succeed in this business if I don't work. I have to work and re-work strategies. I'm not privileged to just get up and leave whenever I think I need a change of scenery."

"Look, here you go again. I know how lucky—"

"No, blessed."

"Well, I know how blessed I am not to have—"

"Never."

"Well, I'm a princess. Is that what you wanna hear?"

"That's more like it."

"Kaye, you work hard. You've built a career for yourself. I envy that. Everything you have is yours. All my life, I've had to rely on others to provide for me. Look at me. I have a master's degree in business management, compliments of my father. I live in a seven-bedroom, four- and-half-bath home on five acres of land, compliments of my husband. I have the finest clothes, dine at the most elaborate restaurants, and I have a nanny on call twenty-four hours a day, compliments of the hubby. So, yes, I am privileged but not at my own hands. I envy you because if anything happens to you where you get fired or you can't work anymore, you'll be able to survive because you've been doing it all your life. If Dre leaves me, I'll have to go back and live with my parents."

"Tori, you are so dramatic. And besides, if Dre ever leaves you, that's what alimony and child support are for."

"Oh, my bad. I guess I forgot. Damn. I do have it all."

"You are so freakin' crazy. You still should have brought my goddaughter. Working long hours, I rarely get to see her."

"I tell you what, take a vacation, and you can spend time with her every day."

"What's up with the sudden interest in going on a vacation?"

"It's not a sudden interest. I've been telling you for the longest that you need a break. You work entirely too hard."

"Well, I don't have any other choice. I have to eat, you know. And besides, I'm on my own. I can't call someone to bail me out."

"Whatever. All work and no play make Kaye a very horny girl."

"I promise you are so stupid."

"Anyway, Dre has one of his clients coming by the house tonight for dinner. Why don't you join us?"

"For what?"

"To serve the food. What do you think, for what? You are so depressing. I've known you for three years and not once in that time have I seen, heard, or smelled a man around you. If you don't get out and have some fun, you're going to deeply regret it later. Besides, it's just dinner."

"I've already explained to you that I'm in a healing process. Since Derrick and I broke up on such bad terms, it's hard for me to trust a man again."

My ex-boyfriend Derrick Hall was a very manipulative man. When we first met, I was so excited. I finally had it all. I was advancing in my career and was going full steam ahead. In the beginning, everything was great. We went out every weekend. We talked to each other every day. I was in love with him, and he was in love with me—or so I thought. As the relationship progressed, we started drifting apart. I remember coming home to my apartment after work one night, and as soon as I opened the door, he started lashing out about how I was a sneaky, lying little whore. Every time I tried to explain myself to him, he would get furious and threaten to leave. He would tell me that if he left, no other man would want me and that I wasn't pretty and the only reason he was with me was because he felt sorry for me sitting alone in Chili's restaurant on a Saturday night by myself. So that was the reason why we were together. Not because he loved me but because he pitied me.

This continued for months. I had lost all my self-esteem. I took the verbal lashings because . . . hell, I don't know why. All I know is that I was in love—dangerously in love. Then one day I went over to his apartment unannounced. When I opened the door, I heard noises. I didn't say anything; I just continued to follow the sounds. When I went to the bathroom and opened the door, there was Derrick and some chicken head in the Jacuzzi tub. I was livid. I started crying and screaming. I wanted her out. She didn't move—she just stared at me like I was in a training bra. So I did the only thing I knew to do: I leaped for the bitch. I was going to whip her ass. I pulled her by the hair out of the tub. She was yelling and screaming, "Derrick, do something, do something." I started punching her in the face. All of a sudden, Derrick jumped out of the tub and yelled, "Get the fuck out," so I was like, "Yeah, bitch, you heard him. Get the fuck out." She looked at Derrick, and Derrick turned to me and said, "Not her, you. How in the hell can you come in here to my house and disrespect my fiancée?"

Wait. Did he say fiancée? How could this be? We'd been dating for months and not once did he ever mention her. Not one picture, not one item of clothing, not one single memento.

My heart shattered into pieces. I looked up, and he was blazing. "I said no, I'm not leaving." I needed answers, and I need them right then. The next thing I knew, he was choking me so hard I momentarily lost consciousness. I remember waking up in the hospital. I don't know how I got there or who brought me. But from that day on, I swore I would never again let a man that close to me. My life, my well-being was far more important than ever being in love.

Tori interrupts my trip down memory lane.

"I understand that, but that shouldn't stop you from trying to find the right guy. He's out there looking for you, and you're hiding behind work. Girl, please. I don't know Derrick, but if he couldn't appreciate you, hell, he didn't deserve you. So why punish yourself?"

"My friend Tori, the hopeless romantic."

"You know you're right."

"Oh hell, well, what's a girl to do?" I say in exasperation. So, what's for dinner?" I ask pryingly.

"Do I look like Betty Crocker to you?" Tori replies flippantly.

"Hopeless. Hopeless."

"At least I got a man. Dinner starts at seven. Don't be late. No sweats, no hoodies, no tennis shoes," Tori replies.

"Great. Now I have to go shopping just to have dinner with my best friend," I say.

"In that case, I might need to go for supervision. You know your ass can't dress worth a damned."

Guess Who's Coming to Dinner?

I love driving to Tori's house. The scenery is beautiful. In the prestigious Buckhead area of Atlanta, the homes are extravagant, some sitting on more than five acres of land with guest houses. I dream of the day when I'm finally able to afford something so precious. Tori doesn't realize how extremely blessed she is. Some people work their entire lives and never even get to see neighborhoods like this.

Pulling up to the gated fence, I enter the code, and the gates open. Every time I come to Tori's place, it seems more immaculate than the last visit. Tori's home includes a great room; a theater room; a family room; a kitchen with top-of-the-line products, which she probably doesn't know how to use; an indoor pool; a gym; and, oh yeah, a guest house.

It's six-thirty, and I don't want to be late and have to hear Tori's damn mouth. I have just enough time to play with Nyla. Before I can even ring the doorbell, Mrs. Happy Go Lucky pulls open the door.

"I thought I told you to get here early," Tori says.

"Tori, I'm here early. It's just six-thirty, and you said dinner was at seven."

Suddenly, Tori looks me over from head to toe and stares me in the face blankly.

"What? What's wrong?" I ask quizzically.

"I thought I told you to come dressed properly."

"I did. The pantsuit is from J.C. Penney, the shoes are Nine West—"

"Girl, you look like you've been shopping at Kmart."

"What?" I question as my self-esteem descends.

"Get in here. We have some work to do. I've told you continuously about leaving the house like a vagabond. I've had enough. Tomorrow we're going shopping. Get upstairs and let's see if I can undo the damage that you've done, dressing like a damn bag lady."

I can't believe she's addressing me like a child. I have to change the subject and do so quickly. "Where's Nyla?"

"Nyla's whereabouts are not a pressing matter right now. We have to get you fixed up."

"Tori, you don't have to be so rude."

"I'm not being rude. I'm just exercising my option on the friend rule."

"And what option is that?"

"A friend in need is a friend indeed." She smirks after making her statement in her cocky little voice.

While Tori is in her department-store closet looking for something for me to wear, her Blackberry starts
buzzing. I answer, and it's Dre.

"Who was that on the phone?" Tori asks.

"That was Dre. He said they'll be a half hour late
because they're stuck in traffic."

"That's marvelous, because you look like a train
wreck."

I look down at my clothes. I don't think I look that
bad. I didn't get any weird stares on my way over. I
reply, "Thanks."

"You're welcome."

"Where's Nyla?" I ask again.

"She's at her grandmother's. Okay, the perfect outfit," Tori says, removing a beautiful suit from her closet.

"Tori, is that a Chanel pantsuit?"

"Why, yes, my dear. You do have some sense of
fashion."

"Are we going out to dinner? I thought you said we
were having dinner over here."

"What difference does it make? You'll never get a
second chance to make a first impression."

"You're so dramatic."

"Somebody has to be. Dressing like you live on a
damn farm."

"I don't have any shoes," I respond in a childlike
manner, ignoring her statement.

She turns around and hands me a pair of silver

Monolo Blahnik slingbacks that complement the lavender Chanel pantsuit.

"Tori, I think this is a little overdoing it."

"Oh, really? So what would you like to put on?" She starts to tap her foot incessantly.

"I'll just go put this on." As I walk to the bathroom, again defeated, I murmur "control freak" under my breath.

"I heard that," Tori shouts. Damn she just doesn't quit. Before long, Tori is yelling at the top of her lungs for me to hurry up. Once I'm through, I open the bathroom door, and her face lights up.

"See how beautiful you look in couture?"

"They're just clothes, Tori."

"Yeah, but see how beautiful you look in couture?" she repeats.

"Yeah. I am kind of sexy, aren't I?"

"Whatever. Let's do something with that sheep wool on your head."

"You mean my hair?"

"Yeah, if that's what they're calling it these days. Let's see how it looks pulled back into a bun."

She brushes every strand perfectly into place and wraps my hair into a ponytail, then secures it into a bun. She adds a clip made of sparkling crystals. "There you go. Don't you look beautiful?" Tori is actually smiling like a mother sending her daughter off to her first prom.

"I feel overdressed." I quickly sense Tori's mood

change. I didn't mean to let that slip out. She doesn't like to be second-guessed.

Tori spins around on her Jimmy Choos, and I swear Linda Blair from the *Exorcist* has emerged. "Look, bitch, you're not going downstairs with me looking like you just stepped out of a soup kitchen. I dress like a supermodel, and if you're going to roll with me, you're going to have to play the part. Is that understood?"

"Yes," I reply, defeated again. Tori always wants me to follow in line. I do it to keep her from getting angry. I know she just wants the best for me.

I guess she's right. She always looks good. Even her workout clothes are couture. If I make it out the house, I feel like I'm doing 100. I really don't think clothes make the person. I believe it's what's inside that matters. I've never been one to dress to impress. I wish Tori could understand that I'm not her.

"Kaye?"

I can barely hear her call my name seeing as how I'm in my own little world.

"Yes?" I reply barely above a whisper. I can tell she knows that she's hurt my feelings.

"We're going shopping tomorrow, and that's the end of it. You're too beautiful to be looking like any regular old skank."

"Did you just call me a skank?"

"No. I was simply making a reference to your choice of clothing, which may warrant a preconceived notion that you may be. Understand?"

"Whatever?" I say as throw my hands in the air.

"Plus, we can take Nyla, since she's the only one you'll spend money for."

"What's for dinner?"

"The hell if I know. Didn't I tell you that I'm not Betty Crocker?"

"Oh, yeah. I forgot."

"Okay. One last thing. Let's put a little M.A.C. lip gloss on for that natural perfection." She sits me down and goes to work on my lips. What feels like hours later, she hands me a mirror. "Voilà! A diva in the making."

As Tori and I head downstairs to the dining room, we are greeted by a delicious aroma.

"Girl, what smells so good?"

"Our chef Simeon prepared dinner."

Suddenly, Simeon pops out of the kitchen to greet us.

"Ladies, ladies, I must say that you are looking more savory than the dinner," he replies in a somewhat disturbing tone.

We both reply with thanks and giggles.

"So, Simmy, what's for dinner?" Tori asks.

"Well, Natori, I thought we would go semi-casual tonight. But now that I look at the attire, I feel as if I should have brought my A-game."

I look at Tori and smirk, "I told you we were overdressed." Her facial expression shows she could care less.

Simeon continues with the menu. "We're having filet mignon with asparagus and potatoes with your husband's favorite dessert, cheesecake with strawberry topping. And of course, Cristal."

"Thanks a lot, Simeon. You're the best."

"No, my darling Natori, that would be you."

"You know what? I think you might be right."

"Anyhoo, ladies, have a pleasant evening," Simeon says as he leaves me and Tori in the kitchen.

And just like that, the cook is gone.

Tori and I walk to great room to talk while we wait for Dre. Only about two minutes pass before the door opens. In walks Dre, and behind him is the most extravagant specimen of a man that I have ever seen. Even though he is dressed in a Phat Farm track suit, he is simply gorgeous.

"Where the hell y'all going?" Dre asks.

Tori looks at me, and I turn away.

"Oh, sweetheart, you know how women love to dress up."

"Uh-huh," Dre responds, unconvinced. "Hey, Kaye. What's up?"

"Hey, Dre," I reply.

"Ladies, this is my client Jalen Matthews. He's a running back for the Atlanta Panthers. Jalen, this is my wife, Natori, but, you can call her Expensive."

"Dre," Tori yells defensively.

"I'm just playing. We call her Tori. And this is her

best friend, Kaylondria Parker, but you can call her Lackey."

"Dre," I say as a roll my eyes. "The nerve."

"I mean we call her Kaye."

"Nice to meet both of you," Jalen responds.

"It's nice to meet you too," Tori interjects. "My husband seems to think he's a comedian."

"Tori, you know I love you and your little friend."

"Damn it, Dre, shut up," Tori screams.

"Why are you so edgy, darling? Kaye understands. Don't you, girl?"

"Of course, I do, you wannabe," I say smugly.

Jalen falls out hysterically. "Man y'all off the chain in here."

Dre then asks Tori what's for dinner. She turns around so quickly, I think I see lightning flash.

"Never mind" is his response. As we all gather to sit down and talk, Tori makes certain that I'm sitting directly across from Jalen.

"So, Jay, my man, how do you think the season is going to look?" Dre asks.

"Man, I'm hoping we can get that ring this year. We were so close last year, I thought I tasted the platinum."

"Dude, you stupid."

I'm holding my own, playing with my potatoes when Tori finally opens her big mouth.

"So, Jalen, are you married?"

"No, I'm not."

"Do you have a girlfriend?"

"No. It's hard being on the road and all."

"Oh, I understand. Do you have a b—?"

"Tori, let's go get dessert," I say matter-of-factly. Once in the kitchen, I look at her through piercing eyes. "I can't believe you."

"I was just making conversation."

"What's up with all the questions? I refuse to believe that you were about to ask him if he has a boyfriend. You have gone totally too far."

"I was just curious."

"Like hell you were. Get the damn cheesecake."

As we return to the dining area, the guys are having a heated conversation over who's the best rapper in the game. Dre likes L.L. while Jalen prefers Jay-Z. I serve the cheesecake while Tori sits looking like a puppy, then she pulls the rabbit out of her ass.

"Guys, why don't we all go on vacation somewhere?"

"Tori, you just had a vacation," Dre informs her.

"Paris doesn't count."

"Since when?" I ask.

Jalen seems to be enjoying himself because he's tickled to death.

"I mean why don't we go to an island somewhere, and you know, chill out."

"Like where, Tori?" Dre asks.

"I don't know. What do you think, Jalen?"

"I actually would love to go on a vacation right

about now. It would be the perfect time to get away before the season starts again, you know to relax and get my mind right."

"Great," I say. "I can take some time off."

"I told you that you needed a vacation. Doesn't she, Dre?" Tori says.

"Yeah," he responds. "Kaye works really hard."

"I would love to keep Nyla till you get back."

Tori's frowns. "What the hell are you talking about?"

"I can keep Nyla while you guys are vacationing."

"No you won't. If anybody needs a vacation, it's you. And that's the end of it. Nyla can stay with her grandmother. She can go on another vacation with us some other time.

Looking totally defeated, I agree.

"Cool," Dre replies. "We'll handle all the travel arrangements."

"But—" Tori tries to interject before Dre jumps in.

"No. Tori, your man's got this."

"So, what are we supposed to do, Dre?" Tori asks.

"What you do best, baby."

We all turn to look at Tori, and she's glowing like she's three months pregnant.

Shopping spree is written all across her face.

Better Shop Around

I'm so excited. I haven't had a chance to see my goddaughter in a week, and I love her so much. Tori is picking me up at my apartment in ten minutes. It's only ten-thirty, so that means we'll be shopping until the stores kick us out.

I hurry downstairs to keep Tori from having to get out of the car. As soon as I get outside, I spot her silver Lexus SUV.

"Hey, girl. What's up?" Tori asks.

"Nothing," I say before turning to my goddaughter. "Hi, my pooh pooh. How's T's special little girl?"

Nyla squeals with excitement.

Tori looks at me and shakes her head. "Girl, if you stop being so depressing you can have a little crumb snatcher of your own and stop trying to horde mine."

"She's a baby, Tori. Not a crumb snatcher."

"Whatever. Get your own shit."

"I promise, girl. You are so trifling."

"Whatever. Get your own shit."

"So, where are we going shopping this time?"

"Hmm. Let me think. First off, we have to hit Victoria's Secret because a sister girl must look good underneath."

If there's one thing Tori and I have in common, it's our love for lingerie. That is the only shopping I love doing with her.

As we pull up to the high-end mall, Phipps Plaza, I scan the parking lot and notice all the high-end cars to boot. Once again, I'm out of my league.

As we park and get out, Tori immediately grabs her Louis Vuitton bag and heads to the opening of the mall.

"What about Nyla?" I ask.

Tori looks at me blankly and states, "You know you're going to pick her up, so why should I bother?"

I grab Nyla's stroller and her Louis Vuitton diaper bag, and we go off behind Tori.

Once inside the mall, I feel like I'm in a totally different place. Everything is so beautiful. The stores have a boutiquish style to them. As I am walking through the mall, I look at all the elegantly dressed people around me, and I look down at my clothes and wonder what I was thinking to come out with Tori wearing a T-shirt and yoga pants. I should have known that she would come to a place like this. No matter what I do, I will never be able to measure up.

First of all, we head into Victoria's Secret. We both buy three sets of underwear.

We leave Victoria's Secret and head to Neiman Marcus. As soon as we get in the store, Tori is off to the shoe department. She is trying on shoes like a madwoman, and eventually settles on a few.

"I can't believe you just spent three thousand dollars on four pairs of shoes," I say as we are standing at the register.

"Girl, please. I caught a good sale."

"What?" I say in shock.

Tori keeps walking through the mall buying high-priced items. Nyla starts getting a little fidgety so I suggest we go and get a bite to eat because it is damn near three-thirty. We stopped at a trendy little Italian eatery called LaBelle's. Tori orders the spaghetti with meat sauce, and I order the lasagna. We talk about all the things that have happened over the past week.

"So, how do you like Jalen?" Tori asks.

"He's okay, I guess."

"Okay? Girl, you must think I'm stupid. I saw how you were looking at him when he walked through the door. You were salivating like a dog in heat. You need to quit fooling yourself," Tori responds.

"So, yeah, he was sexy. That doesn't mean I should jump his bones."

"As long as it's been, not only should you jump 'em, you should also pack 'em up so you can jump 'em again later."

"Tori, you are so relentless." We both let out a laugh. Looking over at Nyla who was every bit of a sleeping angel, we decide to call it a day. Besides, I have to go to work the next day.

Once I say good-bye to Tori and kiss Nyla good night, I go into my apartment. All of a sudden, it hits me; once again I'm all alone. I run a warm bath complete with my Victoria's Secret Pink Freesia Sensual Body Scrub, my usual routine.

I put on my night clothes and kneel at my bed to pray before I allow myself to drift into a peaceful night's sleep.

Going on a Holiday

I am sitting in my office doing research. Drug design is no easy task. I am also trying to put together the paperwork so that my colleagues will be able to continue with my research while I'm on this vacation with Tori. I look up when I hear a knock at the door.

"Come in please," I say to whoever is behind the door.

"Hey, it's just me," my assistant Tina answers.

"How can I assist you?" I ask in a nonprofessional tone. Tina and I have a great working relationship.

"It's actually my job to assist you. I have some more paperwork for you to sign."

"Thanks, Tina," I reply as she places the paperwork on my desk and exits out the door.

What seems like less than two minutes later, the phone is ringing.

"Good morning, this is Kaylondria Parker," I say in my most professional tone.

"Hey, it's me. Tori."

"Yes, madame. What's going on?"

"Oh, nothing. I was just wondering if you want to go shopping today," she says.

"Tori, didn't we just go shopping?"

"Yeah, but that wasn't for the trip," Tori whines into the receiver.

"Girl, I can't just leave work whenever you want to do something. I have a lot of loose ends to tie up as is for this trip."

"I know, but we need to get some things," Tori responds.

"Not today. I really want to have this research set up so it can be tested while I'm away. How about we do dinner instead?"

"Whatever. You and Dre both make me sick. Always working."

"People have to eat, Tori. Let's do dinner at eight. Somewhere quick. How about the deli around the corner?" I recommend.

"No. We need to meet at the mall. I have to pick up some things anyway. Okay. I'll make it really quick. I promise."

"Whatever, Tori. Let's do whatever you have to do expeditiously."

"Great. I'll meet you at seven-thirty."

"Tori, I'll probably just be getting off work. So, I'll leave from here and I'll be tired. I'm not trying to be out all night. See you then. Bye," I say as I hang up the phone.

Tori always wants her way. She's so used to getting it that everybody relents, like I just did, so she doesn't get upset.

I delve back into my work, separating all the designs from all the drafts. I like to keep my drafts just in case I have to start over from the drawing board. This also gives me an idea of how much more work needs to be put forth in this project.

Tina knocks on my door to get my attention.

"Well, if you don't need me for anything else, I'll be going home now."

"No. Thanks a lot, Tina. I'll see you tomorrow."

My boss, William Turner, walks in after Tina leaves.

"How's everything going? Is the development plan coming along smoothly?" William asks.

"Everything is fine. I'm just putting together packets for the rest of the project team," I reply.

"Good. I hear that this new drug will be used by cancer patients for nausea and will be the best thing on the market."

"All the research seems to point in that direction."

"I'm delighted to hear that. Soon, we'll be among one of the top pharmaceutical companies thanks to you. You should be really proud of all your accomplishments here at Alpha. This company probably wouldn't have survived without you. You will be rewarded for all your hard work."

"Thanks, William."

I come from around my desk to walk William downstairs and out the building.

On my way back up to my office, I happen to glance at the clock. It's already seven o'clock. Let me hurry upstairs, so I can meet with Tori.

Once inside of my office, I put all my packets together and put them in my filing cabinet. I lock up and head back downstairs to the parking garage, so that I can meet Tori at the mall.

I'm walking through the mall and like always Tori is nowhere to be found. I reach inside my black Nine West bag for my cell phone to call her. I look on the phone display, and it shows that it is now eight o'clock. It's official: she'll be late for her own funeral.

As I prepare to speed dial her, I hear her voice.

"What up, mami?" I look up and it is none other than Tori with a handful of bags.

"How in the hell could you ask somebody to meet you some damn where and you go off and do your own thing first? You are so rude."

"Heifer, what in the hell is wrong with you? I told you to meet me here for a purpose. You need to put that attitude back in the pot and let it simmer."

"Okay. I'm sorry. I thought you weren't here, and I had a lot of work to do."

"Kaye, you make me sick. You're twenty-eight years old, and all you do is work."

"If I don't work, I don't eat."

"I'm not suggesting that you not work. Girl, you're young. Your whole life will pass you by and you won't have any happiness. You're always worried about other people. That's great, wonderful even, but sweetie, you have to make time for you. Get out and enjoy yourself. No one deserves to be happier than you. What is it for you to accomplish every goal in your life and be alone?"

"Damn, Tori. Are you sure that you have a degree in business management, because that was some straight philosophical bullshit. It doesn't work like that for everyone. What may be accessible for you isn't necessarily what will be accessible for me."

"Kaye, you make everything inaccessible for you. How many times have we been out and some guy has asked you out and you turn him down?"

"Plenty."

"Why?"

"I have to be comfortable in the skin that I'm in. I have to have a mind-set that's willing to take on new things. Right now I'm not focused enough to date."

"Suit yourself."

"Thank you for understanding."

Hopefully that will shut her up for a while about men and dating. She's always trying to hook me up with some narcissistic man.

"You're being very evasive," I say.

"Why do you say that?"

"What are you thinking about, Tori?"

"Nothing. It's just that Dre has found a place where we can all vacation. He called his travel agent, and they decided we should go low-key. No tropical lands, no sunny beaches, no turquoise waters, no Paris."

"Then what?"

"I knew he couldn't be trusted. A travel agent and a sports agent put their minds together and the best they could come up with is a nature trip."

I burst into laughter. It serves her ass right for always recommending ideas that work for her benefit. Finally, Dre has played the coon on her.

"Don't you dare look at me like that, Kaye. You know how I detest trees."

"Tori, *detest* is such a strong word."

"Whatever. I can't wait to see you in the woods.

"Good. You'll be there too, right along with Jalen."

My mouth drops below sea level. I really didn't think she was serious when she was talking to Jalen about going on vacation. She has yet another unofficial title—the comeback queen.

"Tori, I don't think that's a—"

"Who cares what you think? You have no opinion in this matter whatsoever. We're going to South Carolina next week. We'll be living in a cabin by a lake, so that gives us four days to get everything together because we leave Sunday."

"Tori, I still don't know about this. I can't just up and leave my job."

"Honey, sweetheart, oh friend, oh pal of mine, you

are overworked and underpaid. Let someone else pick up the slack for a change. I'm positive that you'll have a job when you come back. You're the one who keeps that company going. No one else is going to sleep at their job but you. So, that's that."

"I don't know if this is a good idea, Tori."

"How could it not be? We'll be having fun together. Since you've been working so much, we barely see each other. I've been doing the mommy and wifey thing so long I could scream. This will be beneficial to us both, you'll see. Like I said, we have four days. We have a whole lot of planning to do, so tomorrow I'll come by your apartment around six to make plans. And oh yeah, I'm bringing Nyla, so see you then."

The mere mention of my goddaughter's name brings a joyous smile to my face. I'm still not sure of this little field trip, but it seems as if everything has already been taken care of. What do you know? I'm going on a holiday.

Are You Ready?

I'm sitting at my desk going over paperwork and when I look up at the clock, it's already three. I can't believe I've let Tori talk me into going on a trip. I can't believe it's already Friday. That means Sunday is the moment of truth. To tell you the truth, I'm nervous as hell. It's been a long time since I've been in the company of a man. I don't know if I can trust myself. What the hell am I thinking? I don't know this man, and he doesn't know me. Tori's even got me leaving work early to plan for some trip.

As I prepare to leave, my assistant enters the office.

"Hi, Kaye. I'm just coming to wish you a wonderful vacation."

"Thanks, Tina. That's sweet of you."

"Girl, you never take a vacation—and no the conference doesn't count as a vacation, so don't even suggest that. You should be like Stella and go get your groove back."

"Umm, Tina, I'm not going to the islands. I'm

going on a camping trip with Tori, her husband, and his friend."

"Quit your lying. You know good and well that Tori isn't going camping."

"Well, her husband planned the trip, and she is."

"No way."

"Yes way."

"This is going to be hilarious. I can't wait for you to get back and give me the 4-1-1. Well, anyway have fun, and maybe if you're lucky, the lion won't be the only thing having fun in the jungle."

"Umm, Tina, I'm going camping, not to Africa."

"Stop it. You know what I mean. So, who's the mystery guy who's going? If he's a friend of that fine Dre, he has to be something to behold because you know what they say: birds of a feather flock together."

"Girl, you are definitely too much. I don't understand why you and Tori don't get along better."

"Please. All Tori does is think about Tori."

"And you think about whom?"

"Okay, I see what you mean. So, who is he?"

"He's a client of Dre's."

"So, he's an athlete. That's big, or is it?"

"Tina girl, if you don't get the hell out of my office…" I say, snickering. We both look at each other and fall out laughing. Tina has proven herself to be a good friend. When I was going through my disaster with Derrick, she was very supportive. I truly love having her around, even if Tori can't stand her.

As I walk out of my office, I tell everyone to enjoy the upcoming week. I make sure that I have all my paperwork and laptop. I've already handed Tina the packets to distribute to the team. I have to work; besides, what else can you do in a cabin for four days?

I'm glad traffic is light. Instead of the usual thirty minutes to get home, it only takes twenty. As I walk to my apartment, I check my mail. Great, no bills, just magazines. I'll have to make sure that I pack them also. As always, Coco is jumping up and down on me as I enter the door. I reach down and rub and her head. On my way into the kitchen, the door suddenly opens.

"Hey, Tori."

"Bitch, I told you to keep your doors locked. If I would have been a murderer, you'd be in big trouble."

"If you were a real person, you would have knocked first."

"Keep getting smart, and you're going to find yourself in a situation."

Nyla gurgles.

"Hey, my sweet. How's T's precious little baby?" I stick my hands out for Nyla, and she reaches for me.

"I told you to get a baby of your own so you wouldn't have to hover over mine."

"But why should I have to go through all that trouble when I can just play with my precious?"

"Hopeless. Hopeless," Tori responds.

"Okay. So what are we supposed to be doing, Tori?"

"Since we're going to live with the coyotes, we have

to plan for groceries."

"Yeah. Oh wait. Hell no. Your ass don't even cook."

"What do you think you'll be doing?"

"Tori, that's not fair," I whine.

"Look, sugar, life isn't fair, but if we dwell on the negatives, we won't be able to enjoy all the positive things that happen to us. Understand?"

"Hell no," I yell.

"Suck it up, Kaye, and let's get started. We have a lot to do tomorrow."

"Okay. First things first," I say, "we need to plan menus. Do you know what Jalen likes?"

"He's a man. He'll eat anything."

"Let me rephrase the question. Do you think he's allergic to anything? I wouldn't want him to croak and then I'd be the most hated woman in America."

"Girl, he's a grown-ass man. He ought to have enough sense to know when something is suspicious. And then again, he might not."

"It's only four days." I sigh. "It shouldn't be that hard."

"I know. Let's just get a whole lot of microwave dinners and make them think that we cooked."

I really have to look at Tori. I can't believe what I'm hearing. She can't possibly mean what she's saying. I see now that I'm on my own with this one, so I quickly change the subject.

"Tori, what are we supposed to do while we're in the middle of nowhere?"

"I don't know. Maybe just chill and have fun. Dre has been so busy lately he hasn't had time for me, so this will be perfect for us. I need some attention, if you know what I mean."

"Let me rephrase the question. What am I supposed to do while I'm in the middle of nowhere and you and Dre are reuniting?"

"Don't be so dramatic, Kaye. Jalen is coming. You can get to know him and just hang out. Talk sports stuff. You love sports, and maybe if you remove a brick from that brick wall that's surrounding your sweet spirit, he might actually enjoy your company, and you might actually have a good time."

I swear I don't know where she gets this philosophical propaganda from, but she is killing me.

"I don't think that I'm unapproachable. I just don't let my guard down for the first man I meet."

"It's not about letting your guard down. It's about trusting. You've let your whole situation with Derrick turn you against all men. All men aren't alike. Don't ever shut your heart down completely. You can't live like that."

"I know that you're right. It's just so hard."

"Well, let this trip be the opening session."

Silence fills the room as I watch Tori take Nyla out of my arms. I really admire Tori. She has everything, and she knows how to keep it. Is happiness really for me? I guess I'll never know if I don't try.

"Why don't we meet so we can go grocery shopping tomorrow? I know we didn't plan, but we can just buy some things and plan from there. Nyla is ready for her nap. She's getting so fussy. We'll have to go in the morning. That way we'll have enough time to pack. And you know I have to approve of everything before you pack it."

"Yes, madea." I laugh jokingly. "How about ten?"

"Sounds good to me. And Kaye, are you ready?"

Let the Games Begin

It's nine o'clock, Saturday, and I still can't believe what I'm about to venture into. I head in the bathroom to take a shower. The water feels relaxing and inviting. I hop out of the shower, dry off, and get dress. I pull my hair back into a ponytail. I have thirty minutes to spare so I turn on the TV. ESPN is on, and they're doing an interview with Jalen.

I linger on every word that comes out of his mouth. I bet women are lined up for miles just to hold his hand. Here, I have the opportunity to spend some time with this man, and I'm tripping. I vow from this very second that I'm going to have a wonderful time, and that's it.

The doorbell rings. I go to answer it, and before I can turn the knob, Tori bursts through the door. Coco jumps off the sofa and runs toward the door and starts barking like she has lost her mind.

"Hey Coco," Tori says to Coco as she rubs her head and Coco jumps up and down like she has no home training.

Then she turns to me and says, "Good morning. Are you ready?"

I have to laugh at her before I respond. "Bitch, I told you about walking into my house.".

She smiles and states so perfectly, "But I rang the doorbell this time."

Apparently Coco thinks this is acceptable because she sits at Tori's feet and looks at me like I've just said something wrong.

"You see," she says pointing to Coco, "the puppy doesn't think I did anything wrong."

"Well, that wouldn't be a problem if Coco paid rent, utilities, and put food on the table. She is only here as a source of comfort and she's tipping the line by consorting with the enemy."

I look at her as she lays by Tori's feet looking a little too cozy for me. It's time she recognizes which side her bread is buttered on. "Coco, my dear, mama loves you with all her heart and her soul, but if you don't start acting like you know who's the boss I'm sure there's a pound nearby that would love to take you in."

Coco's ears point toward the heavens as if she has just receive the epiphany of her life and she quickly flees from Tori's feet to stand beside me as if the thought of being left in a pound is way more than she can bare.

"Oh how cruel. I'm going to call PETA on your ass and let them know how you threaten poor helpless animals. I'm sure they can think of just the right punishment for you. Evil as hell. Have you seen *The Wizard of Oz?* Houses have a tendency to fall on evil people."

"Girl, let's get out of here before I say something that I'll regret. Where's Nyla?"

"She's already off to Grandmother's house."

We get into the Lexus and drive to the market. As soon as we enter the door, Tori walks off and start to browse on her own. "Tori aren't you going to get a shopping cart," I ask her as she continues to walk away.

"No, you can go ahead and get it."

"Tori, you really need to stop. You can at least push a cart."

"I just got my nails done," she replies as she continues to walk towards the magazines.

"So, you can pick up magazines but you can't push a shopping cart," I ask her as I grab the magazine out of her hand and place them back in their spot. "We came in her to shop and that's exactly what we're going to do.

We head to the produce aisle and we grab lettuce, onion, tomato, apples, and bananas.

"What type of meats are we getting," Tori asks

"Steaks, hamburger, roast, pork chops, and some breakfast foods."

"Okay, Let's also get potatoes and some rice," she says as she heads to the boxed dinners aisle.

By the time we leave out of that store, we have a

grocery bill of two hundred and fifty dollars. I hope that Dre and Jalen can at least make breakfast. I can't see myself cooking three meals a day for four days.

As soon as we walk in my apartment, Tori goes straight to my bedroom. She starts rummaging through my closet. I sit in silence because I already know what she's doing. She is getting my wardrobe together. She has packed my whole line of Juicy Couture, two pairs of Monolos (both gifts from her), and all my lingerie.

I finally get a chance to ask her something that has been on my mind since she first thought of this trip. I didn't want to ask her before because I didn't want to show interest, but under the current circumstances, I don't see a reason why I shouldn't.

"Tori, what's Jalen really like?"

"Where is all of the sudden interest in Jalen coming from?"

"I just thought if I'm going to be spending time with him, at least I deserve to know something."

"Well, let's see...Jalen is twenty-nine. He's single. No kids. He's very spiritual. He was raised by his grandmother. He was neglected by his father and his mother who turned up right before he went pro. He still loves her. He's very sociable—a jokester even. I hear he's quite the cook. And rumor has it, he's very talented in the art of pipe laying."

"It never fails. We were having a perfectly good conversation and there you go bringing up trivial stuff."

"How is that trivial?"

"Never mind, Tori." I can just hear her snickering inside. "Laying pipe doesn't make a man, character and substance do."

"Well, go ahead and put him down for those too." This time she laughs uncontrollably. "Anyhoo, I have to be going. I still have a few things to gather, and I need to get plenty of rest. There's no telling what we may encounter on this trip."

"Love you," I say.

"I know," she responds.

As she leaves, I sigh in a relief. Let the games begin.

Fantastic Voyage

It's Sunday. I decide to go to work after church to tie up some loose ends. I love to go to work, so going in on Sunday doesn't really bother me. It's the one place I feel secure and in charge.

As I start to put on my jogging set, the phone rings.

"Hello," I say.

"What up, chick?"

This would be Tori.

"Good morning, Tori. What has you bright-eyed and bushy-tailed this morning?"

"I was just calling. Thought about you. Trying to make sure you don't back out on me at the last minute."

"Umm, Tori—"

"You know how you are. Every time we decide to do something together, you back out at the last minute."

"Umm, Tori—"

"So, I'm calling to make sure that you understand

that no matter what, there is no plausible excuse to get you out of this one."

"Umm, Tori. Tori," I say, exasperated, "I have to go to work."

I hang up in her face. We go through this charade every time her feeble little mind comes up with some brilliant idea. I'm really not up for this.

I look at Coco who is looking at me as if she's waiting for me to inform her who was just on the phone. I look at her and instruct her to go to the kitchen where I put some food and water in her proper bowls. Although she's still looking like she expects an answer. I don't give her anything. This is my house. I run this. Nosey bitch.

I rush downstairs and jump into my Camry and drive northbound to the expressway. I turn on the radio, and the Terror Squad's "Lean Back" comes blaring into the speakers. I change the channel to the gospel station, and Yolanda Adams is belting out a tune. Now that's better. I have to get my mind right.

After I enter my building and I reveal my ID to the guard, I ride the elevator to the sixth floor. I never could have imagined that working for an up-and-coming drug research center would be so tedious. I love being a research chemist because it allows me a chance to help others. I am also thankful and blessed because the job has allowed me to have a high-end five figure salary and thusly afford a nice quality of living.

As soon as I enter my office, the phone rings. It's

Tori.

"Girl, what are you doing?"

"Something you know nothing about."

"What?" Tori asks

"Work, Mrs. Thing."

"You just can't get enough, can you? Today is Sunday, and you're at work. Not to mention the fact that you're supposed to be getting prepared for the trip. I think Jalen is going to call you today."

"Whatever gave you that idea, Tori?"

"Well, he came by earlier, and he asked about you. Since he was so concerned, I told him to call you."

"Tori, Tori, Tori, you need to find a hobby."

"I already have one, Kaye."

"And that would be?"

"To find your sexually repressed self a man."

"Thank you for being so caring."

Just as I'm about to check my desk to make sure that everything is in order, my cell phone begins to ring.

"Tori, I have to go. I have to take another call, but I'll call you later."

"Okay, but don't forget," Tori says.

I answer the phone. "This is Kaylondria Parker."

"Hey, Kaye, what's up?"

I'm totally perplexed because I have no clue who this smooth-talking man on the other line is.

"Hello," I say hesitantly.

"Oh, it's me, Jalen. Tori gave me your cell number.

I hope that was okay. I tried to reach you at your home number, but there was no answer."

I'm thinking, *Why does this man have all my numbers?*

"Hi, Jalen. I was actually on the phone with Tori, and it's not a problem. So what's going on?"

"Nothing. I was just trying to make sure you were still going on the trip. Tori said you might change your mind. I don't like being a third wheel."

"No, Jalen, I haven't changed my mind. I'm actually looking forward to going. It'll be a trip in itself to see Tori become at one with nature." We both laugh at that statement.

"She'll be fine. We won't be in the woods per se. We actually rented a cabin that has all the amenities of a spa, so she'll be right at home. It's more like a retreat."

"Damn. I thought for once in her life she was going to have to rough it."

"Now you know that girl would never make it in the wild."

"I know, I know."

"Anyway, I just wanted to touch base with you and make sure everything was cool. I'll see you tonight."

"Sure, Jalen, see you then."

I don't believe I allowed Tori to talk me into going on a trip. I don't know if I'm ready for this.

My cell phone rings again, and of course, it's Tori.

"You can't follow instructions at all. I told you I'd

call you back."

"Whatever. I knew you would forget. That's why I called you first. Are you ready?"

"Ready for what?"

"The best time of your life."

With that said, I look out the window and ponder the possibilities. I'm interrupted by Tori's yelling. "I hear you, girl, and yeah, I'm ready," I say.

"Good. We'll pick you up at seven. Be ready and comb your nappy- ass head."

"Tori, my hair is always combed."

"Whatever. I'll see you at seven."

As I see it, this will be one trip to remember. I walk over to my mirror on the other side of my office and stare at the image I see and ask, *Are you ready*? The image just looks back at me, dumbfounded.

What Dreams May Come

I finally make it home from the office at five-thirty. I finish packing. I gather my tan Juicy Couture sweat suit and Nike tennis and lay them on the bed. I fully plan to be comfortable during the ride. I have less than two hours to get ready, so I put the bags that Tori packed by the front door and then hurry to take a quick shower.

When I get out of the shower, it's six o'clock. I begin to put on my outfit. My hair is now wet, so the best I can do is pull it back and put it in a ponytail. I then put on a baseball cap. I finish packing trinkets like magazines, novels, and puzzle books. I put my laptop in my bag and set it next to the door. I go to the kitchen and grab a bottle of water.

Coco is looking sad because she knows that I'm leaving. I hold and play with her for a while. "It's okay, sweetie. Mama's going away for a little while but I'll be back soon. Sarella is going to check on you from time to time and take you for walks. You'll be okay." She just lays in my arms and pouts. It almost makes me want to cry.

The kitchen door swings open, and I turn around to find Tori standing in my foyer rolling her eyes. "What?" I say nonchalantly. She doesn't respond. She just starts to grab my bags and heads to the SUV.

As I begin to pick up purse, I see Dre and Jalen coming through the door. They each grab the bags from Tori, and I silently close and lock the door behind us.

"So, are you excited, Kaye?" Dre asks.

"Yeah, I'm pumped up." Tori turns around from the front seat and gives me a glare that would weaken a murderer. "What?" I ask her again. Still no response.

"Yo, check this out, ladies. This is going to be bananas," Dre declares.

"Dre, what in the hell are you talking about?"

"Having fun, Tori."

She ignores Dre altogether and begins to talk to Jalen.

"So, Jalen, you like Phat Farm, huh?"

"Yeah. I like to chill and relax, and their sweats are real comfortable."

"That outfit looks good on you."

"Thanks."

Now, I get it. She's mad because I have a hat on. She ignores me and is now talking to a third party, which happens to be Jalen.

"I took a shower before I left and my hair got wet,

so I just put it in a ponytail and put a baseball hat on," I say to no one in particular but for Tori's benefit.

"I think you look hot," Dre exclaims.

"Me too," Jalen concurs.

I smile nonstop. Tori just pulls the mirror down and rolls her eyes at me again. I put my head down in disgrace, and when I look up I see her putting on lip gloss, smiling at me. Whew! Off the hook.

When we get to the expressway, I realize I haven't eaten anything all day. I am starving but we're already en route so I don't say anything. Dre is blasting the new Ludacris CD. Jalen is reviewing what looks like football plays. Tori is looking through DVDs. I grab my bottle of water and a magazine and hope for the best.

We ride for about two hours, and then Dre says he is pulling over to get something to eat.

He and Jalen decide on McDonald's, which is perfectly fine by me. Tori and I go in to get the food while they go next door to get gas.

They make it back as we're exiting the restaurant. Tori gives Dre his food so that he can eat and drive. I give Jalen his. He smiles at me and says thank you. My heart begins to flutter, and a warm feeling begins to invade my soul. I immediately start to relax. This may not be so bad after all.

"Tori," I ask, "are you going to put in a DVD?"

"Sure, if you want me to. What do you guys want

to watch?"

Dre shouts, *"Big Rump Shakers III."* Tori ignores him and puts in *Belly* as Jalen finishes eating.

"Are you full?" I ask.

"Yeah. I'm just a fast eater."

After about thirty minutes of watching the DVD, Tori, Jalen, and I fall asleep for what seems like hours.

When I finally awaken, I see Tori is every bit of the sleeping beauty. Jalen is dead to the world. This gives me and Dre some time to talk.

"Dre, do you want me to take over so you can get some rest?"

"No, ma. I'm fine."

"If you get tired, just let me know."

"Okay, but I'm fine. So what do you think about ol' boy."

"He's cool, but you know I'm not looking for anything right now."

"I understand. That shouldn't stop you from enjoying yourself, Kaye. You work hard nonstop. You're a very beautiful and intelligent woman. Any man would be lucky to have you on his arm."

"I'm not a trophy, Dre."

"It's not about being a trophy. It's about completion. Every man wants a woman to complete him. A lot of women don't understand that. Y'all go into relationships expecting too much too soon. Everything comes in its own time."

"That's exactly why I don't try."

"Kaye, you can't compare one man to the next. All men aren't alike. Don't let one bad relationship set the standard for every other one. If you go into anything expecting the worse, that's probably what you'll end up receiving."

"Do you think my standards are too high?"

"No. I think your expectations of men are too low. You need to let go of that bad relationship and stop carrying all that negative energy around."

I chuckle.

"What's so funny?"

"Tori thinks the same thing."

Before I know it, we pull into the driveway of this enormous cabin.

"I thought cabins were small?" I question.

"Not all of them," Dre responds.

Dre wakes Tori up, and I nudge Jalen. He stirs but doesn't wake up, so I take my bottle of water and pour just a tidbit on his cheek. He jumps up quickly and hits his head on the TV screen in the headrest. I burst into laughter.

"That's not funny. You're going to regret that."

"I'm sorry. I couldn't help it."

We all unpack the Escalade and start heading toward the cabin.

"This is beautiful," Tori shouts.

"Shh, before you wake up the wild animals," I tell her. She quickly runs to Dre, and we all fall out laughing,

"Hah, hah," she says.

Jalen opens the door, and we're greeted by a warm fire and candles lit everywhere. The cabin is immaculate. There is a calming waterfall in the middle of the wall across from the fireplace and a mink rug on the floor in the middle of the room. We go on a tour. We enter the first bedroom, and it has a king-size poster bed with a plasma screen.

"Are all these cabins this gorgeous?" I ask.

"Yeah," Jalen responds. "This is the only one with three bedrooms though. They all have the same basic design."

Tori comes back from her personal tour. "Dre, how many bedrooms is this cabin supposed to have?"

"Three," he replies.

"Umm. There are only two and a huge bathroom."

"What? I can't believe this. I specifically asked for the three-bedroom cabin that we saw online," Dre yells.

"So much for Internet shopping," I say.

"Let's not worry about that," Jalen responds. "We'll work out sleeping arrangements. This cabin is too fly to complain. There's a Jacuzzi on the patio and a whirlpool bathtub in the bathroom. We'll be okay. This will not ruin our vacation. Dre and Tori, take the first bedroom, and Kaye, you take the other one. I can sleep in the living room on the pullout sofa."

"No, I can't allow you to do that, Jalen. You are an

athlete and you need to be able to sleep comfortably," I say.

"It's okay, really," Jalen responds.

"I have an idea," Tori states. "Why don't you guys share the bed? It's huge. You'll never know the other one is on the other side."

"I have a better idea," Dre interjects. "Why don't you guys take turns sleeping in the bed?"

"Perfect," I say. "If that's okay with you, Jalen."

"Yeah, that's cool."

"Then it's settled. Good night, everybody. It's late, and I'm exhausted," I say as I stretch out my arms.

Tori and Dre take their bags into the bedroom, and Jalen and I take ours.

"You can have first call at the bed. I'll be fine in the living room. It seems peaceful in there," Jalen tells me as he heads back into the living room.

"I know, but I just want to make sure that you'll be okay. I don't want your back to go out and you to blame me for it. I can't afford to pay you your million-dollar salary."

"Kaye, you're hilarious. I'll be fine."

As I proceed to head back to the bedroom to get some sleep, Jalen interrupts my walk back.

"What the hell is that?"

I listen, and I hear bumping and noises. "Oh, that's just the lovebirds. It didn't take them long to get reacquainted. Well, since it seems like I'm not going to get sleep for a while, do you want to help me unpack the groceries?"

"Sure. I want some fruit anyway."

We head to the kitchen and begin to put away the groceries. Jalen grabs an apple, and I grab a handful of grapes before I gather blankets and pillows to fix him a spot on the sofa.

"Thanks, Kaye. You're so nurturing."

"You know, I try."

"So tell me a little about yourself. I know you're a research chemist. What else makes Miss Kaylondria Parker tick?"

"Okay, here it goes. My name is Kaylondria Parker. I'm twenty-eight years old. Single. No kids. I'm a research chemist for an up-and-coming pharmaceutical company. I haven't dated in two years. I love to read."

"Wow, that sounds really exciting. These are all the things I already know," he says as he is yawning and waving his hand in front of his mouth. "So really, what do you do for fun?"

"I work a lot. I really don't have time for fun. So tell me about you, Mr. Football."

"Well, besides the stuff you probably already know, I'm a real laid- back dude. I like to do the usual stuff."

"The usual stuff?" I inquire.

"Clubbing, vacationing. I'm a real movie buff. I don't have any kids. I'm single. I love my moms. Other than the football gig, I'm a normal guy."

"I'm sure the ladies think so."

"The females come with the territory. You just have to deal with it."

"So are you a self-professed playboy?"

"Nah. I just chill."

"I'm sure," I say as I begin stretching again. I look at my watch. "Wow, it's one–thirty already. I'm going to go ahead and call it a night. See ya in the morning."

"For sho."

With that, I head back to my big lonely bed. As I pass by Tori and Dre's bedroom, I realize they must be sleeping because the noises are non-existent. Sometimes I wish I could have someone hold me through the night. What dreams may come?

It's a Beautiful Morning

I awaken to loud laughter. I turn to look at the clock. It's nine–thirty. I can't believe I've slept so long. I'm usually wide awake by now. I jump out of the bed and look out the window, and it's beautiful outside. I open my bag and decide to put on some Seven jeans and a key hole top. I then head to the bathroom to freshen up.

After I'm dressed, I walk in the kitchen, and everyone is eating breakfast.

"How come you guys didn't wake me up?" I ask.

"You were sleeping," Tori said.

"Thanks a lot, Tori."

"Kaye, do you want some breakfast?" Jalen asks.

"No, I'll just eat a grapefruit."

"So what's on the agenda for today, ladies?"

"Dre, you guys planned the trip so why are you asking us?"

"Tori, I was just trying to be polite."

"Is there a place we can go to get some fresh air?" I

ask.

"Why don't we go soak up some of nature's fresh air?" Dre asks.

Everybody agrees, so after breakfast, we all decide to go outside and take a walk around the grounds. We meet and greet some fellow vacationers on the way.

When we return from our stroll, we see that it is already noon.

"Umm, why don't we prepare for lunch? I saw a grill on the patio. You guys could grill some chicken breasts or some steaks. Tori and I could do some side dishes," I say.

"I'm really not the cooking type but I'll go outside to the grill with Dre for moral support," Jalen says.

"Thanks a lot, dude. You're such a generous liar," Dre responds. "Jalen actually cooks a little."

"Oh really," Tori replies as she takes out some vegetables and hands them over to me.

While the guys go outside to prepare the chicken breasts, Tori and I make side dishes in the kitchen. I look at Jalen as if he is the chicken breast.

"Stop salivating," Tori remarks with a snicker.

"Sorry, Tori. He's divine. I never knew a man could look so good in jeans, and he's dripping with the sauce of sexuality."

"Woe, taste and see if he's good."

"What? Girl, you need to quit. I was just joking."

"That's it, Kaye. You say you're joking but I know in your heart you mean it. I think Jalen likes you. You can at least just try to see if he's good. Hell, get your feet wet. Don't put your heart into it, just your body."

"You make me sound like a loose woman. It has been a while, but what if I don't remember how to? My body does need it—no, my body deserves it."

"That's my girl."

Lunch was wonderful. The guys decide they want to get into the Jacuzzi, so Tori and I go to my bedroom to get dressed. I decide to go for a one-piece with the sides cut out while, of course, she puts on a two-piece bikini. We then go outside to join the fellas who are already drinking and listening to rap music.

I jump in followed by Tori. As soon as she gets in, Dre begins to kiss her passionately.

"Get a room," I state.

"You know what, Kaye? You are so right. Come on, Dre. Let's go to the bedroom. Bye, guys."

"Bye, Tori," Jalen and I respond simultaneously.

"Alone at last," I exclaim nervously.

"Yeah. This feels great. You know this is good therapy for my body. This is usually what I use after a game. The season is so rigorous it can wear a man down."

"What a life. Do you ever get tired—I mean do you ever feel like quitting and resuming a normal life?"

"Hell no. I watched my grandmother work her fingers to the bone. My career has allowed her to have the life she deserved before she passed, and now my mother is back, and she gets to see that I turned out alright. I won't let anything jeopardize that. My grandmother sacrificed so much for me. I could never go back to that life."

"I understand. I'm sure she's so proud of you. It must be so fulfilling to be able to give your mom so much and then be able to live the life and do the things you dreamed of when you were a little boy. It's amazing."

"Hey, but you're not doing too bad yourself: a black woman who has her own, now that's impressive. So many women expect guys in my position to be their savior. It's really unfair. A lot of guys can't handle the pressure, and it's too much responsibility, so they bow out."

"I think that most guys get into relationships for one thing, and when it gets hot and heavy, they bounce. As women we take in a lot of things. The emotions for us are totally different than the emotions guys feel. It's more spiritual for us. For guys, I think it's a release of all the stress that has been manufactured all day, so once that pressure is gone, you no longer feel the need to stick around; that is, until the next release is needed."

"The mentality is different, I think, Kaye. Women expect so much. It's so hard sometimes to fill the expectations. Theoretically, we're doomed before the relationship gets off the ground."

"Maybe. I don't know, Jalen. It seems like sometimes we're alone in this struggle, and that's the part that hurts."

"I feel you. So what do you look for in a man?"

"Understanding, strength, determination, restraint, intelligence, and respect."

"Wow, what a lengthy list."

"Not really. Those are just the basics. Further into the relationship, I require that he heal the sick, raise the dead, change water into wine 'cause ain't nothing like a good party, and he must be a prolific orator."

"What about walking on water?"

"Damn, Jalen, I think that's a bit too much to ask for."

"Oh, really? Girl, you are so hilarious. Tori never told me that you were this fun to be around."

"Speaking of which, we might need to go and check up on them before they kill each other. Besides, we've been in this water entirely too long. It's almost three o'clock."

Jalen gets out of the Jacuzzi first and holds a towel for me. I can't believe how well this is going. My psyche is becoming enthralled with him each moment we spend together.

I go inside and put on some yoga pants and a T-shirt. When I come out Dre and Tori are sitting on the sofa watching a movie, and Jalen is lighting the fireplace.

Tori looks up at me and says, "Don't you look refreshing."

I politely roll my eyes and sit on the chaise. Jalen sits on the edge of my chair and begins to rub my feet.

"So, what have you guys been doing while we were taking a nap?" Dre smiles at his own comment.

"What nap?" I reply. "You guys were so loud that the wild animals practically came out of hibernation. We were, if you must know, in the Jacuzzi where you guys left us talking."

"Yo, Jay, were we really that loud?"

"Yeah, man, y'all were kind of loud."

"Whatever, haters. Y'all in here pretending like you haven't been having a good time. You have Jalen in here rubbing your feet. You looking a mighty bit cozy to me," Tori says.

"My beloved Tori, mind your own damn business."

"No, you didn't, Miss Fast-Tail Heifer. Dre, I think you need to keep a closer watch on your boy. He definitely has something up his sleeve—or shall I say his pants?"

"Alright. Alright, you guys. That's enough. We've just been hanging out. I thought this was the whole idea, to get us away so we can enjoy ourselves. That's what we've been doing, so give us a break," Jalen says in our defense.

"Well said, my man. Chill out, honey. I think it's cool that Jalen and Kaye are becoming acquainted with each other. Let's call a truce. So what are we going to do tomorrow?"

"I think we should go shopping," Tori suggests.

"Umm, Tori, we're in the middle of nowhere. Or have you forgotten?" Dre retorts.

"Hell no, I haven't forgotten. When you told me we were coming to this God-forsaken place, I looked on the Internet for surrounding sites, and there's a mall about an hour from here. Let's all get to going because I need some down time," Tori proclaims.

"Tori, please explain to us, dear child, how you are going to have down time at a mall that is surrounded by mobs of people?" I ask.

"Girl, please, when I'm shopping, no one else exists in my world but me, so let's go tomorrow."

We all decide that we would go with Tori's suggestion and go to the mall the next day.

Everybody says good night as we all prepare for a long day with Tori.

When I wake up the next morning and get dressed, I find Tori sitting in the living room watching TV.

"What are you doing up so early?" I ask.

"I'm ready to go shopping. Why aren't the men up yet?"

"I don't know, Tori." I join her in watching TV.

The guys finally make an appearance at one o'clock.

"Oh, looks like somebody was really tired last night, huh?" I say to Jalen.

"Yeah, yeah, whatever. We're up now, and that's all that counts," Dre states, unconcerned.

"So, are you ladies ready to head out?" Jalen asks.

"Thought you guys would never wake up. I just started to leave without you. That's what I should have done. I probably have missed all the sales."

"What sales?" Dre asks.

"Sweetheart, I always bargain shop."

"Since when?" Dre asks seriously.

Tori cuts her eyes at him and heads toward the door. We all follow her before she goes ranting again.

Once we actually get to the mall, we realize that it's a strip mall. This little known fact doesn't seem to bother Tori in the slightest.

Jalen has been quiet since we left the cabin. I wonder what he's thinking. I've been really enjoying his company. I haven't been this comfortable with a man in years. It seems almost surreal.

"Okay, gang, mostly chicks—or mainly Tori."

"Dre, you make me sick," Tori yells.

"Are you sure?" he asks.

"Absolutely," she replies.

"Then I guess you don't want my bank card, huh?"

"Of course not, beloved. I have a duplicate."

"Girl, you are sick. I do believe that they have some anonymous meeting that you could attend to break that habit," Dre teases.

"It's not a habit. Just an indulgence," she remarks

"Whatever," Dre states.

The strip mall is actually kind of nice. It doesn't have any of the high fashion stores that Tori loves to frequent, but it is nice just the same.

Tori immediately leaves us in her dust. Dre follows reluctantly. Once again Jalen and I are left alone. We walk quietly behind.

"So Kaye, tell me the truth—the honest-to-God truth."

"About what?"

"Why don't you have a man?"

I can't believe he has the audacity to ask me that question. "Well, I don't have a man because I'm busy with my career. Most of my attention has been placed on that. That's my number one priority right now."

"You mean to tell me that you're so busy you can't find just a little time for some romance?"

"To tell you the truth—the honest-to-God truth—Jalen, I just got out of a bad relationship. It's only been two years. I need time to get my perspective back. I wasted totally too much time and energy in that relationship only to come out wounded."

"Sorry to hear about that. I understand the need for a healing process, but when do you determine that it's time to get back in the game again?"

"I don't know. I guess I'm supposed to wait for that feeling."

"What feeling?"

"You know, the nervous energy—the man who makes me feel giddy."

"Have you even been on any dates lately?"

"Well, no."

"Then how are you going to ever get that feeling again?"

"I don't know. It's still too soon."

"Listen. No one can ever get into your heart if you have a brick wall guarding it. No one said being in love was easy. You just have to keep trying until you find that one person who makes you happy."

"I know, but once you've been hurt, it's hard to trust again. Some days I look at Tori and Dre, and I want a family terribly, then there are times when I think about what I went through, and I'm completely terrified."

"All men are not alike. It's so true what they say. One man can make one woman hate all men."

"I know, and I don't want to be like that. I really want to know what real love is. It just never seems to work out for me."

"It will, but you can't give up."

"Okay. I won't."

"Good."

There's something about Jalen that makes me smile inside. I haven't felt this way in a long time. I must admit that it feels good. Maybe too good.

"So, are you hungry, Kaye?"

"Yeah, a little."

"Let's find the guys and see if we can get some dinner."

When we turn around, up walk Tori and Dre. To our surprise, Tori doesn't have one bag in hand.

"What happened? Are the stores closed?" I ask

quizzically.

"Nope." Tori replied.

You didn't buy anything?" I ask as I see Dre giggling away. "What's so damned funny?"

"I'm turning over a new leaf," Tori exclaims.

"Whatever. Let's go. We're starved," I say as I turn around and continue walking.

"Where do you guys want to eat?" Dre asks.

"I don't know, man. Let's go for something quick," Jalen answers.

"I got an idea. Let's order some pizza and talk about sex," Tori suggests.

"Tori! Never mind. Okay, Tori, you order the pizza now so by the time we make it home it should be ready," I suggest.

When we pull up, the driver pulls up also. Dre pays for the pizza, and we all run inside to get comfortable.

"So, what movie do you guys want to see?" I ask

"It doesn't matter." Tori exclaims. "I'll just put in *XXX*."

Dre and Tori dig into the pizza first.

"Okay. It's time for some intelligent intellectually stimulating adult conversation," Tori says.

"You mean sex," Dre says, laughing.

"Of course. So Miss Thang, when was the last time you engaged in some adult-oriented exercise?"

"Tori, I promise you are absolutely out of your mind."

"Answer the question," Jalen badgers.

I know the hell he didn't just ask me when was the last time I had sex.

"It's been that long?" Dre questions.

"Why all of a sudden are you all interested in my love life?" I ask, becoming irate with the whole lot of them.

"Or lack thereof," Tori remarks snidely.

"Go directly to hell, Tori."

"Calm down. Calm down. We're just concerned," Dre interjects.

"I'm sure."

"It's okay, baby. Jalen understands," he says as he rubs my back in a circular motion.

"Thanks, Jalen."

"Umm-hmm," Tori says suspiciously.

I just totally ignore her.

As we finish watching the movie, Tori and Dre are cuddling on their way to the bedroom. Once again Jalen and I are alone. I look up at him sitting in the chaise. This is the first time I notice all his features. I don't know if it's because of the candlelight or the way the moon casts a glow on him through the Venetian blinds, but his face is chiseled. A work of art— thick lashes, square jaw line, light brown eyes, and caramel skin. His lips are thick and full. His buffness can be attributed to his profession. His legs are long and muscled. His feet...Damn. I don't have any business staring at this man's feet. I look up in total amazement to see him looking up at me. I smile.

"What's on your mind?"

"Nothing."

"Really?"

"Nothing. I was just thinking."

"About?"

"Nothing. I mean I was just thinking."

"Kaye, it's okay."

"What's okay?"

"To wonder what it would be like."

"What what would be like?"

"You know what."

"Jalen, I don't think that's a good idea."

"Kaye—"

"No, Jalen. Good night."

"Good night, Kaye."

Whew. That was real close. I'm glad I was able to pull myself out of that situation. I've got to get a better hold of my emotions. I've got to be more prepared or this man is going to make me lose control. I head to the shower and prepare myself for another day.

It's Getting Hot in Here

The next morning I wake up to the smell of a wonderful aroma. After I tidy up in the bathroom, I head straight for the kitchen.

"Good morning, sunshine."

"Good morning Jalen. Where is everybody?"

"Oh, they left."

"Left? Where? When?"

"They headed out late last night. They caught a cab to the airport. Nyla was rushed to the emergency room."

"Is she okay? Let me get my things together, and we can be out of here in no time."

"Kaye, Tori and Dre called this morning. Nyla is fine. She had a slight ear infection. Her temp went up. That's why her grandmother rushed her to the hospital. They gave strict instructions for us to stay. Besides we're leaving tomorrow anyway. Just sit down, have breakfast, and relax. We can call them later."

"I don't know, Jalen. Maybe we should just leave

now. What are we going to do here by ourselves?"

"I don't know. I'm sure I'll think of something later. Just relax."

"Okay. I'll try. Let me just call Tori to make sure everything is okay."

I head back into the bedroom and grab my cell and dial Tori's number. I get her voicemail, so I leave a message.

When I return to the kitchen, Jalen is sitting at the bar eating.

"I called Tori. She didn't pick up. I hope everything is alright," I say, worried.

"I told you she called and said everything was fine," Jalen states to reassure me.

"She could have at least woke me up to tell me she was leaving."

"She said she didn't want to worry you. I'm sure she'll call back in a little while."

"How did I sleep through all that?"

"That happens when youre body is tired," he says as he looks at me. "Are you hungry?"

"Famished," I say as I lick my lips.

"Good. Have some breakfast with me."

"I didn't know you could cook. You said you didn't cook."

"Well, I do a little something. I actually have a cook at home, so I don't do much."

"Liar. It looks like you can throw down," I respond as I look at the feast before me.

I take some pancakes, sausage, and eggs and add them to my plate. He wasn't kidding. The breakfast was wonderful.

"So, Miss Lady Love, what do you want to do on our last day?"

"I guess I could get some work done."

"No work. This is a vacation."

"I know. I know."

"How about we go to the spa and hang out, then we can go and have a nice meal?"

"Okay. That sounds great."

"Oh, I'll make it sound even better. It's all on me."

"In that case, not only do I want a massage, but I'm also going to get a facial, manicure, pedicure, and aromatherapy treatment."

"Now you're beginning to act like Tori."

"Oh, whatever. What woman wouldn't want to be pampered, especially if the man is paying?"

"Oh yeah."

"Oh yeah. As a matter of fact, let me get dressed right now."

As I leave, I hear Jalen laughing. He might just be okay. Being friends won't hurt anything. I go to my room to pick out something to wear to the spa. I grab my Juicy Couture jog set. I can't believe how meticulous I'm being about what to wear. Tori isn't even here. Her influence stretches beyond her presence. Jalen's right. Tori is beginning to rub off on me. I pull my hair back into a ponytail and clip it with a butterfly clamp.

When I walk out of my room to meet Jalen, I see him sitting in the living room with his Sean John sweat suit on. It's definitely going to take more than a massage to keep my nerves from rattling. Mental note to self: Don't forget to kick Tori's ass for leaving me here with this fine man.

"Okay. I'm ready to go."

"I see. You look very relaxed.

"Yeah, I'm trying to get my mind prepared already."

"Kaye, you are so crazy."

We both head out the door and jump into the SUV. As soon as he turns the ignition, 50 Cent is blaring through the speakers. I politely reach over and turn the music down.

"Oh, you're not fan of 50?"

"I like 50 a lot, but at low decibels. I think you've killed all my viable ovaries."

"I hope not. The world deserves to have a bunch of little mini yous running around."

"Is that right?"

"Yeah, that's right. Just relax. I'm really getting tired of telling you that. I think we're going to have a good time, even in the absence of Tori and Dre. You need to get from under Tori's shadow before she brainwashes you completely."

"Jalen, I totally resent that. I'm my own person. I make my own decisions. I don't need Tori around for self-assurance."

"Yes you do. You linger on everything that she says.

I understand she's your friend and her opinion matters, but what do *you* really want?"

"Tori is my best friend, and I do value her opinion. It's because she's my best friend that she knows and understands what's best for me, even when I can't see it."

"I hear ya. It's just seems like it's time to come into your own."

"Wow, and all this time I thought I was living my life like it was golden."

"Yeah, but still, get out of that cocoon and live a little."

"Okay. Just for you, Jalen. Don't you care what your teammates think of you?"

"Hell naw. I live for me and me only. When it all boils down to it, I'll be answering for all my actions, not them."

Pulling up to the spa, my mind is in mid-flight. I think about all the things I've been through these last few years. I've been hurt so many times it seems now that I just step back and pray that nobody notices me. Jalen's right. I have to get out of the dungeon that I've built for myself and live a little. I'll do just that, and I'll do it today. "Jalen," I say.

"What up, ma?"

"It's kind of hot in here."

Breathe, Stretch, Shake, Let It Go

Walking into the spa, I am totally mesmerized. The theme is a tropical paradise. Fountains are everywhere. There are waiters going around serving drinks. Jalen puts his hand in the small of my back as the technician approaches us.

"How may we service you today?" the attendant asks.

"Deep–tissue massage," Jalen responds.

"And your wife?"

"Oh, we're not married," we both respond simultaneously.

"Well, that's a pity because you two make a lovely couple."

I give a faint smile, hoping not to be too obvious about how uncomfortable her remark makes me. I assume that Jalen thinks nothing of the comment because he is scoping out the place.

Feeling a little antsy, I say, "What about a hot stone massage, facial, French manicure and pedicure." If he's going to pretend I'm not here, he might as well get the visual with his next credit card statement.

"Oh, you want the diva treatment? Right this way. Follow me," the attendant says as she leads me to a room in the back.

As we're walking away, I glance back to see Jalen in the middle of a swarm of chicken heads escorting him to the back room. Hmm, just like that, already forgotten. Why didn't I take my ass home?

Oh, my God, the stone massage is wonderful. It seems that with each placement of a stone onto my back, a weight has been lifted. Maybe this was a good idea, I realize as I'm finally being escorted to my next treatment.

"What kind of facial would you like?" the aesthetician asks.

Suddenly, I'm dumbfounded. I know not one thing about facials. "If Aveeno doesn't make it, I don't worry about it," I reply sheepishly. "What kind do you offer?"

She smiles, pats my hand, and says, "Don't worry, sugar. Ms. Mona is going to take good care of you."

Somehow that isn't reassuring as I look at the wicked grin that is painted across her face.

Ms. Mona takes me to the spa therapy room and prepares me for my facial. While I'm receiving it, Tori calls.

"Hey, heifer. What's going on?"

"Tori, my mother didn't raise any cows."

"Since when?"

"Anyway. How's Nyla?"

"Is that all you think about? You didn't even ask me how I was doing."

"Okay, my bad. How's the evil, twisted mother of my wonderful, sweet, and innocent-unlike-her-mother goddaughter doing?"

"Keep it up. Just keep it up. I'm fine, and Nyla's doing okay. She's out of the hospital, and her fever is down. She's resting as we speak."

"Great. I was going to come home this morning, but Jalen advised me that you guys said you wanted us to finish out our vacation."

"And?"

"And what?"

"How's the vacation?"

"It's going fine. I'm at the spa right now."

"Oh, shucks. I can't believe your cheap ass is putting money on your appearance."

"I'm not. It's compliments of Jalen."

"Did you give him some last night?"

"Some what?"

"Don't be crass, Kaye. You know what I'm talking about."

"Unfortunately, Tori, we're all not hookers at the point like you."

"Girl, you best be trying to put a deposit on that."

"For what?"

"So you can withdraw it later."

"Tori, stop it. Besides, I don't even think Jalen likes

me like that."

"And why do you say that?"

"Because anytime another woman approaches him, I become invisible."

"Maybe because you make yourself invisible. Kaye, a guy like Jalen likes a woman who takes interest in herself. You have to stop trying to hide behind your hurt. It radiates in the inside; it doesn't have to radiate on the outside. When men see that, they become apprehensive in approaching you."

"I know, but I can't compete with them."

"You don't have to compete. You're a remarkable person and a phenomenal woman. That's what draws a man to a woman. That's what creates the bond."

"You did it again."

"Did what?"

"Found a way to make it seem like I'm worth the trouble."

"Because you are. You just don't see it yet."

"Thanks, Tori."

"That's what friends are for. Let's talk about the spa. What's happening?"

"I'm getting a caviar facial," I say all excited.

"Shut the fuck up."

"Tori, watch your language."

"Okay. Okay. My bad."

"Goodness. I'm going to get a manicure and a pedicure too."

"Great. Since Jalen is paying, you might as well get

an aesthetician to put some color to your face and do something to that nappy-ass head of yours."

"Tori, how much is all this going to cost?"

"What do you care? Not enough to put a dent in Jalen's wallet."

"You're sure he won't mind?"

"I've seen Jalen spend more on alcohol. He won't care. By the way, where is he?"

"Getting a deep-tissue massage and God knows what else by the neighborhood skanks."

"Whores can smell money a mile away."

"No kidding."

"So, what are your plans for tonight?"

"I don't know. Maybe a movie."

"I promise, you are so pathetic."

"What?"

"Girl, find something to do. You're going to have to take the initiative."

"Okay."

"Don't be afraid to let Jalen sample the goodies."

"What?"

"Stop being so innocent, Kaye. You're a woman and Jalen's a man. When a man meets a woman, he—"

"Tori, shut up. You are so nasty."

"You better recognize. Men like Jalen come once in a blue moon. If I'm not mistaken, the next one is scheduled for the next millennium. You better hop on that. Literally."

"I suppose that's how you got Andre."

"Nose wide open."

"Tori, you're relentless."

"Say whatever. You know you're in a drought. You need to be planning accordingly. With all the dust you got stored on that—"

"Tori, I'm warning you."

"So, you already know."

"It's just that I don't think he likes me like that."

"Just stand back and see."

"Okay. But—"

"But nothing. Just relax. I gotta go. Nyla is awake."

"Kiss her for me."

"I swear I should have let you breastfeed her."

"Bye, Tori."

"Bye, Kaye."

I laugh to myself. Sometimes Tori's antics can be outrageous, but I know she means well. Maybe she's right. If Jalen makes the first move and only if he makes the first move...I won't pursue him like those hoochies do. I guess it's okay for me to indulge myself sometimes, right?

I'm too confused. I just lay my head back as three women scuttle around me—one for the pedicure, one for the manicure, and one for the color consultation. I try to relax, but I can't. All of a sudden, I hear Pastor Mase blaring from the speakers, "Breathe, Stretch, Shake, Let it Go." I guess I'll do just that.

Where the Party At?

I can't believe it. I feel so energized. I look absolutely radiant. I think I'll start wearing makeup more often. I even buy two hundred dollars worth of beauty products. Tori will be ecstatic. I wonder if Jalen will feel the same way.

I'm waiting in the lounge area for Jalen, and he finally appears— surprisingly alone. Chicken heads removed. He just walks right past me to the front desk to Ms. Mona. She smiles and points toward me. I wave kiddylike. He looks absolutely shocked. He walks toward me. I subconsciously reach out and hug him. Damn he smells good.

"Kaye, I'm sorry. I walked right past you."

"Yep."

"You look...you look so..."

"Grown and sexy?"

"Yeah."

"So, I guess you like."

"I like."

"Yeah, I hope so. Remember you paid for this."

"Money well spent."

"Thanks a lot, Jalen."

"You're welcome, sweetie."

After the valet brings the Escalade around, Jalen reaches out and opens my door. I hop in and watch him walk around to the driver's seat. I also spot the C-note he places in the valet's hand and the young boy's excitement. Great gesture. Maybe Jalen will be okay after all.

"So, Miss Lady, what do you want to do on our last night together?"

"I don't know. Maybe catch a movie?"

"Naw. We can do that anytime."

"Okay. Hmm. Hmm. Let's see. Hmm. Hmm."

"Damn, Kaye."

"What?"

"It's taking you entirely too long to find something to do. Let me ask you this. What do you really like to do?"

"I like to go to the movies."

"Out."

"I like to read novels."

"Out."

"I like to watch movies."

"Already said that one. Out."

"Okay. Okay. I guess I'm boring," I say

Jalen begins to laugh hysterically.

"Why are you laughing so hard?" I ask.

"Because you are too cute."

"Oh yeah? If I was so cute, why did you walk past me in the spa?"

"Are you kidding? I didn't even recognize you."

"You think?"

"I thought you were a sex kitten."

"Jalen, be for real."

"I am. I was peeping you."

"Uh-huh. So you wasn't peeping me when I was an ordinary girl?"

"Nah, it ain't like that. So, back to the matter at hand. What do you want to do tonight?"

"Jalen, I don't know. I don't get out much, and I'm not really a party girl."

"Do you drink?"

"No. I don't like it."

"Have you ever had a drink?"

"No."

"Then how do you know that you don't like it?"

"I just know."

"That settles it. We're going to the club and we're drinking."

"But, Jalen—"

"But, Jalen, my ass. It's settled."

"Yes, papi."

"You ain't know?"

When we get back to our cabin, I start looking through my things for something to wear.

Unfortunately, I can't find anything to put together for the club. I decide to keep my hair in the pin curls the beautician at the spa left it in. I look in the mirror, and I must say, I do look sexy, but I still can't find anything to wear. I do the only thing I know to do—I call Tori.

"Hey, Tori."

"Hey, girl. What's happening?"

"Girl, you wouldn't believe what Jalen told me."

"Do tell."

"He told me that he didn't recognize me because I look like a sex kitten."

"Get out."

"And then he said that he was going to take me to the club tonight, and he was going to make me drink."

"And you agreed?"

"I had no other choice. At least that's what he said."

"G'on, girl."

"One problem."

"How in the hell do you do that?"

"Do what?"

"Always find a but in the midst of a promising situation."

"Tori, this is serious. I don't think I have anything to wear."

"I told your lame ass to stay out of Target, but you never listen, and now there's this fine man who wants to take you out and you can't even—"

"Tori, okay. I get it."

"Okay. Remind me what we packed?"

"Jeans, sweaters, and jeans."

"As far as tops."

"T-shirts, button-downs…"

"What about all the clothes I put in from when we went shopping?"

"Well…there's that shirt by Roberto Cavalli."

"Kaye, that's a dress."

"Are you sure? I think it's a shirt. Has to be. There's not enough material for a dress."

"Totally clueless. Kaye, wear that dress over some jeans, and put on some heels."

"Okay."

"And Kaye?"

"Yes…"

"Comb that nappy-ass head of yours." *Click!*

Nappy head. What is she talking about? My hair is not nappy. Is it? A look in the mirror for confirmation. Checking the edges. Checking the ends. No my hair isn't nappy. I just got it done. Tori is just trying to clone me into her. I will not allow it. Nonetheless, I still have to find something to wear to the club.

After much toiling, I decide to put on the Roberto Cavalli shirt (no matter what Tori says, there is no way this can be a dress) and my Seven jeans with my Steve Madden sandals. I go to mirror in the bathroom to check my makeup. I add a hint of Beaux M.A.C. lip gloss and voilà, the finished product. I'm sticking to the philosophy that less is more. I glance down at my watch and notice that it's eleven o'clock. I hear Jalen knocking at my bathroom door.

"Who is it?" I ask, already knowing.

"Who are you expecting?"

"LL Cool J," I say coolly.

"Sorry, baby girl. You set your expectations entirely too low, so you're stuck with me—the equivalent of a Greek god."

"Oh my goodness, you are so vain."

"Hardly. Just accepting the fate that was handed to me."

"Incredible."

"That's me. So are you ready?"

"I guess."

"Are you going to open the door?"

"Maybe."

"What's holding you back?"

"I'm afraid of the monster."

"What monster?"

"Mainly the one that's behind the door."

"Girl, if you don't bring your ass up out there, we gonna have some issues. I'm ready to get drunk as hell."

"Are you planning on drinking and driving?"

"Kaye, open the door and let's go."

"I need to know this before I venture out with you. Safety is a must. And besides, friends don't let friends drive drunk."

I hear him snickering. He must really think I'm crazy. I finally open the door, and Jalen's just staring at me.

"Don't look so hard. You may get cross-eyed."

"Tori got you dressed, huh?"

"Tori's not here. Why do you say that?"

"Because your breasts are hanging out of your shirt."

"It's not a shirt. It's a dress."

"Then why do you have on jeans with it?"

"It's the new style. If you give me a second, I can go back and change," I say, embarrassed.

"Nah. You straight. Let's roll."

"Okay," I respond as usual.

I'm watching Jalen as he maneuvers through traffic, and all of a sudden I wonder how he really feels about me. Seeing him stare at my breasts made me quiver with delight, but I wonder if he could really have feelings for me.

He turns the radio on and "Where the Party At" blares through the speakers. I look at Jalen, he looks at me and grins a wicked smile.

"Yo, ma?"

"What up?"

"We're about to tear the club up."

I arch my eyebrows in a quizzical form. "Jalen, I ain't staying up all night. No way, no how."

"Just wait," he replies and starts singing with the radio. "Where the party at?"

We pull up to the Posh Club. Jalen parks the

Escalade, and we get out and head to VIP. The bouncers let us in. No security check. It's interesting how when you have money all the rules seem to be broken.

As we head into the VIP section, which is actually upstairs, I look down to see all the people dancing to "Headsprung." When Jalen appears, he's bombarded by females—or what I like to refer as chicken heads. I stand back to watch his interaction with these women. I be damned if he doesn't walk away with those whores as if I don't exist. Typical Negro.

I find a seat to watch all the scantily clad women throw themselves at Jalen. I look at my watch, and it's nine-thirty. I wonder what time this place closes.

I look up and I see a guy staring at me. I smile. He winks. He begins to move toward me. I shift in my seat as I watch him get closer.

"Hello, beautiful," he chimes.

"Hi," I respond.

"So, what's a beautiful lady like you doing all alone in a place like this?"

"Just chillin'," I say ghettolike, never letting on that I'm not alone.

"So, can I buy you a drink?"

"Sorry. I don't drink."

"Don't apologize. I was just trying to be a gentleman."

"Thanks anyway."

"How about a dance then?"

"I don't know. I'm not really a great dancer."

"Neither am I. Let's go."

He extends his hand, and surprisingly I take it. He's not as handsome as Jalen, but he's just as dapper. He's dressed in Roca Wear with black Cole Haans.

As he leads me to the dance floor, I search for Jalen, but I don't see any sign of him. The club is totally packed. There's wall-to-wall booty shaking. I still can't believe Jalen left me like that. I can't wait to see him so I can give him the tongue lashing that he deserves.

Soon as my feet touch the dance floor, T.I.'s "Bring 'Em Out" blares through the speakers, and everybody bumrushes the dance floor. I am totally out of my element.

My partner grabs me by the waist and begins to grind on me. I relax and begin to dance with him. We end up dancing so much that I'm almost completely soaked.

He takes me back upstairs. I'm exhausted and dehydrated. I need something to quench my thirst. He must be able to tell because he guides me straight to the bar. He orders a Hypnotiq and an apple martini for me. Reluctantly, I take the drink as we make our way to sit down.

"Oh, by the way, I'm Lamont."

"I'm Kaye. Nice to meet you."

"The pleasure is definitely all mine," he says in a suave voice.

As we begin to explore each other in conversation, Jalen walks up and interjects, "Are you ready?" I glare at him. How dare he check me after that stunt he just pulled?

"Oh, hi Jalen. This is Lamont."

Jalen looks up at Lamont and looks back at me and states in a matter- of-fact tone, "It's late. We have to get up early tomorrow."

I nod to prevent a confrontation. I turn to Lamont and say, "It was nice meeting you, and thanks again for the dance." He nods in agreement and walks away.

Jalen then grabs my hand and pulls me toward the exit before I can get a word out. I can barely keep up. The bouncer halts us at the entryway because of some sort of confusion. I feel someone slip a small piece of paper in my hand, but things are so crazy I can't see who it is. I immediately place the paper in my hand-bag, knowing it has to be Lamont.

I'm fuming as we exit on the expressway.

"What's the problem?" Jalen asks snidely.

"What's the problem? What do you mean what's the problem? You couldn't have been any more rude, could you?"

"What are you talking about?"

"Lamont."

"Who's Lamont?"

"Lamont. The guy I was talking to in the club."

"Oh, you mean the guy you was almost sexing in the club?"

"Jalen, we were just dancing."

"If that's what you call it."

"I know you're not talking with all the chicken heads who were surrounding you. I didn't even think you knew I existed."

"I knew, and I was watching. That's why I had to rescue you."

"Rescue me from whom, Jalen?" I question, irritated as hell.

"Yourself."

"Well, thank you, Captain Save a Hoe."

"You're welcome. For your information, if you must know, I was signing autographs and meeting some people for publicity. And you can deposit that piece of paper he gave you in the trash."

"How did you see that?"

"I see everything."

I watch his face. He seems somewhat agitated. If I didn't know any better...couldn't be. I'll be damned. He's jealous.

We pull up to IHOP and get out and head toward the restaurant in silence. I look for some kind of reaction in his face. He's totally stoic.

"So what do you want to eat, baby girl?"

"I don't know. Let's just eat at the buffet."

We head to the buffet, and the aroma begins to permeate through my soul. At that very moment, I begin to realize just how hungry I am.

I fill my plate with fruit, eggs, pancakes, and sausage. Apparently, Jalen's appetite is just as ferocious as mine. He loads his plate down with pancakes, eggs, sausage, bacon, grits, and French toast. He is eating as if the food is going to sprout legs and walk off the table.

"You might wanna slow down. You know you might get choked."

"Ha, ha. So, baby girl, tell me what you think about me."

"You are so vain. Everything isn't about you."

"Of course it is. So tell me."

"Hmm. Let me see. I think you're a callous, cold-hearted, good-for-nothing, low-down, dirty, loose manwhore."

Jalen spits out his orange juice and looks at me in a confused state with his mouth wide opened.

I fall into laughter.

He smiles. "Okay, you got jokes. We'll see. We'll see. You're definitely paying for this," he says as he points to the food.

"No, fair, Jalen. You didn't even pay for us to get into the club."

He looks back with those sexy bedroom eyes and winks, then states, "Because I can do that."

Jalen and I continue talking about life and what we hope to achieve out of it. I learn that he wants to become a sportscaster one day and maybe even invest in a team of his own. We talk for hours. I tell him about my research and how one day I want to even start designing my own fragrances.

"Wow, Jalen. I'm glad you convinced me to come out tonight. I really had a good time."

"Good. You need to start getting out more. I promise night life won't contaminate you. It'll just make you relax a little more."

I look up at him and smile. I'm totally smitten with this man. "Are you ready to go?" I ask.

"Yeah," he responds. "Oh, by the way, I haven't forgotten. You're still paying the bill."

I look at him and laugh as I leave the money for the bill and follow him. I look at my watch, and it's now two-thirty. I'm totally exhausted and can't wait to get back to my comfy bed.

"Jalen, what time are we leaving in the morning?" I ask.

"Let's shoot for twelve, that way we can get some rest."

"I can't wait to get home. I'm so worried about Nyla."

"You wasn't worried about Nyla when you were out on the dance floor bouncing that ass."

"Here we go."

"Damn right, Little Miss Innocent."

"Jalen, I was just dancing."

"Yeah. Yeah."

We walk to the door. Jalen opens it with his key. I immediately begin to take off my shoes. Jalen turns around and smiles.

"What?"

"Just because you bought me breakfast doesn't entitle you to free reign of these good loins."

"You are definitely vain," I say as I head to the shower, undressing the entire time. This is absolutely what I need. I turn on the jets and step in. The water is almost therapeutic as it hits my skin. The body wash begins to awaken my senses. I feel rejuvenated all of a sudden. After about ten minutes, I jump out and dry off. I put on my PJs and head toward the bedroom when I notice Jalen lying on the couch watching *Sports Center.*

"Even when you're not working you're working, huh? Or are you just in love with seeing yourself on TV?"

"Nah, I just love sports. I thought you was tired."

"I was, but after my shower, I got a bolt of energy."

"Then join me."

At his request, I sit beside him on the sofa. He flips through the channels and finally decides on BET. Videos are on. R. Kelly's "Ignition" remix is playing. Jalen jumps up and grabs my hand.

"Let's dance."

"I don't know, Jalen..."

"Oh, so you won't dance with me, but you'll freak some chump in the club?"

"Do I detect a hint of jealousy?"

"Yeah. Let's dance."

"You are so spoiled," I say as I grab him around the waist. It's at that moment that I know. I am totally attracted to Jalen. He's grinding and rubbing me all over. My body is tingling. He has awakened desires in me that I haven't felt in a long time. He turns me around so that my back is against his chest as we bounce, bounce, bounce, bounce to the music. I can't believe what is happening. I feel Jalen's nature begin to rise. He is smelling my hair. We never even realize when the station cuts to a commercial. He turns me around again. I gaze deeply into his eyes. I can't hold back the lump in my throat.

"Jalen," I sigh heavily, trying to hold back my sudden desire.

He puts his finger to my lips and shakes his head. "No, Kaye. No excuses."

How did I get myself into this situation? I could scream. He leads me into the bedroom. I'm terrified. I'm not ready for this. I begin to think so hard that my head is spinning. How can I get myself out of this?

I watch Jalen as he fumbles for the radio. My hands begin to sweat. I hear Brian McKnight in the background making promises he can't possibly keep.

I continue watching Jalen as he removes his shirt. Oh my God. He has muscles everywhere. There's a whisper in my right ear: "You're making a mistake." Another whisper in my left ear: "Go ahead, girl. You deserve this." I'm totally confused. I can't think straight.

Jalen walks toward me, beckoning for me to come closer. He extends his hand. I just look at it. I am paralyzed with fear. He moves closer. He's so close I can smell the maple syrup still lingering on his breath.

"Kaye," he whispers.

"Yes," I respond.

"I want you," he replies. "Now."

"Jalen, I…"

Before I can finish my sentence, I feel his tongue inside my mouth. I taste his meal. The maple syrup is so sweet. His kisses are so tender. I want to stop him. I will my mind to stop him. My body just isn't listening.

I feel his hands pulling on my top. I grab them. He pulls me closer. Kisses me deeper. I never even realized that not only is my top off but my bra is also removed. Damn he's good. He picks me up and places me on the bed, never releasing his tongue from exploring me. He unbuttons my jeans and pulls me toward him. What am I doing? This can't be happening.

"Jalen, we're moving too fast," I weakly protest.

"Baby, life is what you make of it. Let go," he replies.

"Don't hurt me, Jalen."

"I just want to please you."

"Okay," I reply innocently as I try to push back all the fear and uncertainty swirling around in my head, causing my temples to ache.

He separates my legs. I gasp for air. I feel as though I'm suffocating. He crawls up me like I'm a ladder. I inhale. He kisses my neck. I exhale. He travels down my body, planting kisses, covering every spot. He reaches my navel. He licks. He travels back to my breasts, exploring my nipples, sucking for nectar that won't come. I am overfilled with emotions. I moan at the pleasure he is extending to my body. More moans escape my soul.

He continues to place kisses everywhere on my body, traveling down until he reaches my dead end. He looks at me with starry eyes.

"Jalen," I gasp.

He says nothing as he begins to let his tongue speak for him. I shudder. It's been so long since I felt like this. I squirm, but he's firm, not letting go as I hear the sucking and smacking sounds he makes with his lips. My body jerks in uncontrollable spasms. I scream in ecstasy. He moans, never stopping his deep investigation of my abyss.

The spasms become quicker, the moans louder, the licking more intense. I grab his arms, trying to hold on to him for fear if I let go he'll consume me.

"Jalen," I shout. "Baby, please…"

He says nothing, still letting his tongue speak for him. My body tenses as I sit up and release the explosion that he has created inside me. Finally, the release.

He looks up at me. Silence. I watch as he unbuckles his Sean John jeans. I watch as they fall to the floor and he steps out. I watch as he sends the Calvin Klein underwear to meet the jeans. Mass hysteria. He is fully loaded. There is no way in hell I'm letting him stick that thing in me. I'll need medical attention when he's finished.

He senses my anxiety. He covers my body with his, kissing me passionately on the lips. We do this dance for what seems like an eternity. I begin to relax. I never prepared myself for what was next. I lost focus in all the attention he was giving my lips.

He thrusts inside of me. My body shakes from the unexpected action. No hint. Just action. I moan, not just because of pleasure but also because of pain. He is massive. The room spins as he works his way in and out of me, willing my orifice to him as if he already owns it. My hands travel down to that spot to relieve myself of some of the heat and pressure when I realize he's not wearing protection.

"Jalen, stop," I say in panic mode.

"Shh, baby, this feels good."

"No. Jalen, stop."

"What's wrong, baby?"

"You're not wearing anything." I crawl from up under him, eager to hear his response. He pulls his hands to his head.

"I don't got nothing. I didn't bring anything with me. You got something?" he asks me.

"No, Jalen, I don't. We can't do this without protection."

"Don't you trust me?"

"Jalen, I barely know you."

"Kaye, come on."

"Jalen, I don't know…"

"Relax, baby. Everything will be okay."

"How can I be sure?"

"I've done this before. I'll pull out."

I'm sure that he has. I look at him, not quite sure, but I can't escape the desire building up inside of me. I nod in agreement.

He reenters me, sending shock waves to my brain. The grunts and moans that escape us are reverberating off the walls. We do this dance for what seems like an eternity. Twisting, turning, rocking the boat until finally the pressure is much too great, and we both shudder together in release.

I turn over, and tears stream down my face. Jalen has broken his promise. He explodes inside of me. Too tired to converse, our bodies relax into a steady state as our breathing evens out. I fall into a trancelike sleep, only to be semi-awakened by music. Sounds like angels. I concentrate harder to make out the melody. I can't. It couldn't be. Damn that sounds like the theme music from the *Titanic*. My body finally succumbs to sleep, and all thoughts are left to ponder for the next day.

After the Morning After

Iawaken to sunlight glaring in my face. I turn to face Jalen who is still sound asleep. I look at the clock. It's ten-thirty. I get up and head to the shower. I then put on my traveling clothes—yoga pants, T-shirt, and tennis shoes.

After getting dress, I decide to call Tori. There's no way I can possibly tell her about last night. I just have to talk to somebody.

"Hello."

"Hey, Kaye. What's up? Are you guys on your way back?"

"Well in a little while. Jalen is still sleeping. How's Nyla?"

"Girl, she's fine. She's still asleep."

"That's good. I was really worried about her."

"I know. Sorry to up and leave you like that, but I didn't want you to have to cut your vacation short. So how was your day alone with Jalen?"

"It was cool. I'm ready to leave though. I need to

get back to work."

"Well, okay, but stop by here as soon as you make it home."

"Okay." And that's the end of the conversation. I can't believe she didn't pry. That is so unlike Tori.

I hear shuffling in the bedroom. Jalen's awake. The morning after. I exhale slowly. No matter what, I have to face him.

I walk into the bedroom. "Good morning, sleepy head," I say.

"Good morning," he responds, obviously still sleepy.

He walks to me and gives me a hug. I breathe in the scent of him, hugging him tighter, not wanting to let go.

"Are you ready?" he inquires.

"Yes. I'm all packed."

"Let's go. Just give me a few minutes to get myself together."

We pack our bags into the SUV and drive off. He turns the music up loudly. I squint from the thunderous roar.

What's up? You don't like Luda?"

"Yeah, I do actually, but at low decibels."

"My bad."

He turns the radio down and focuses on the road. The silence is so loud. I wonder if he'll broach the subject about what happened last night or if I'll have to do it. My hands are sweating because I'm nervous as hell.

I don't want to give him the impression that I'm a woman who frequents one-night stands. I also don't want him to think I'm being too needy, so I sit back and exhale.

"Why are you always doing that?"

"Doing what?"

"Deep-breathing like that."

"I'm sorry. I was unaware of my actions. It's actually a relaxation technique I use to channel stress."

"What are you stressing about?"

"Nothing."

"Last night?"

"Well not really stressing, just thinking."

"You didn't enjoy yourself?"

"Jalen, you know I did."

"Then, why the stress?"

"Uncertainty."

He pauses as if he's contemplating his next move, carefully choosing his words.

"Kaye, I've had a wonderful time with you. I'm glad that we were introduced to each other. I don't think that I'm ready for a relationship, but, we can still kick it. I'll be cool with that."

My only response, "I hear you." I mean what can I say? What should I expect? I let him have just what he wanted. Why do I always seem to promote the I'm-so-lonely role? I guess some habits die hard.

We ride in silence.

"Are you hungry, baby girl?"

"Yeah."

"I'm gonna have to stop and get some gas. What do you have a taste for?"

"I don't know. It really doesn't matter, as long as it's good."

"Let me get some gas first."

He pulls into a gas station and immediately gets out and heads to the pump. I go into the store, looking for a magazine or a book of some sort to get my mind off what happened last night. I need a constant distraction so Jalen won't be able to read my expression. I grab three magazines, pay for them, and head back to the SUV where Jalen is already waiting.

He informs me that there's a burger joint where he wants to eat. I nod in approval.

I'm happy when we get back on the expressway, and I see that we are only an hour away from home. I feel as if I'm suffocating. I don't know why I'm so surprised that he isn't interested in a relationship. I should have seen this coming. Oh well, live and learn—or in my case, live and learn and learn again.

"Why are you so quiet?" Jalen asks, breaking the silence.

"I'm reading."

"You've been reading since we left the gas station."

'I know. I like to read."

"Kaye, it's okay. Why do I feel like you regret what happened last night?"

"I don't regret it, Jalen. I just feel like I should have

waited. I don't want you to have preconceived notions about me."

"Like what?"

"That I'm loose."

"Kaye, I know you're not loose," he says as he's suddenly thrown into a bolt of laughter.

"Why are you laughing so hard?"

"Just your terminology. Relationships take a whole lot of work. I'm busy with football. Always on the go. I'm not ready to be tied down.

"I'm not trying to tie you down," I respond.

"I'll tell you what, let's just chill and see where this takes us, okay?"

"Okay," I reply.

When we pull up to my apartment, I feel relieved. I'm exhausted, and I want to sleep in my own bed.

"Well, here we are, safe and sound," Jalen exclaims.

"Thanks for bringing me home, Jalen."

"You're welcome, baby girl. Let me help you with your bags."

He retrieves my bags and follows me to my apartment. As soon as we enter, my dog jumps up and down, happy to see me. I pick her up and notice that Tori has fed her. Jalen sneaks up behind me and takes Coco from me.

"Oh, what a cute mutt?" he says as he twirls Coco around, shaking her.

"She's not a mutt. She's a shitzu, and her name is

Coco."

"What's up, Coco?" he asks her as she begins to rub her nose against his face.

"Hmm. That's interesting."

"What's interesting?"

"How she's taking a liking to you. It usually takes a couple of visits for her to warm up."

"What can I say? Ladies love me."

"Yeah. Yeah," I say, waving my hands in the air.

"Well, since I see that you're safe and sound, I'm gonna head on out." He begins to walk toward the door and Coco follows him.

"Bye, Coco," he tells her.

She begins to whimper as he opens the door.

"Hey, Kaye?"

"Yeah."

"Let's go out tonight, do something like catch a movie and go to dinner."

"Sure." Now he wants to catch a movie.

"Pick you up at eight."

"Okay. Coco, come to Mama." She totally ignores me and continues to follow Jalen. I actually have to pick the little bitch up and rush Jalen out the door. How does he do that? Does every female and female dog bask in his presence? Obviously.

At six o'clock, I begin to prepare for my date with Jalen. As I head into the bathroom, the phone rings.

"What up, chick?" I answer the phone all ghettolike.

"Ooh. What's gotten into you?"

"What are you talking about, Tori?"

"You seem so peppy. When did you get in, and where's Jalen?"

"We just made it in a few hours ago."

"Un-huh."

"What?"

"So, what did you all do?"

"We went to the club. Oh, Tori…"

"Yeah."

"Let me call you back."

"What? How in the hell are you going to act as if you don't have time to talk to me?"

"I know. I know. I'll explain later."

"You better, and next to the Bible, it better be the greatest story ever told."

"You don't have to be so dramatic, Tori."

"Whatever. Later."

I hang up the phone and prepare myself for my date with Jalen.

I take a long shower. I am excited. Maybe Jalen does like me and he's just feeling me out to see how I'll react in different situations.

At 7:45, Jalen rings the doorbell. I barely get the door completely open before Coco is on his tail.

"What's up, Mocha?" Jalen says to Coco who is jumping up and down his leg.

"Her name is Coco."

"Isn't that like the same thing?"

"No," I say sternly.

"Oh, well. I don't really think she minds."

I look at Coco, and she's giving me the puppy-dog look like I just said something stupid. Oh well, I guess the bitch doesn't mind.

"I'm ready. Let's go. Bye, Coco. Mama will see you later, okay?" She begins to bark uncontrollably. "So where are we headed. Jalen?"

"I don't know. What do you have a taste for?"

"Umm. I don't know."

"I hate indecisiveness."

"It's not like you know what you want either."

"I do. I was just trying to be a gentleman and let you decide first."

"Oh, really?"

"Yeah. Really." He pulls into this restaurant that is actually a steakhouse.

As we are seated, he looks at me with knowing eyes. Not sure if I wanna know what he's thinking, I ignore him and look over the menu. The waiter takes our order, and I feel Jalen staring at me.

"Take a picture," I say, trying to be a smart ass. He reaches for his phone and immediately snaps the shot. Damn technology. "Why are you staring at me?"

"I'm admiring you, not staring."

"Oh. My bad. What's up, Jalen?"

"You're just different."

"Different from what?"

"All the other chicks I've been with."

"How so?"

"You're just different."

"Is that a good thing or a bad thing?"

"It's just a thing."

Just a thing. What the hell is he talking about? Men. They never know what they want.

Dinner is actually great. It has been a while since I've had such an extravagant meal, especially with such an extravagant man.

"So, what's next, baby girl?" Jalen asks as the waitress brings the check.

"Thought you wanted to take in a movie. It's ten o'clock, so we'd have to catch a late one."

"I got a better idea. How about we go to Blockbuster and rent something?" Jalen suggests.

"That's fine, Jalen, but where will we watch them?"

"How about at the store?"

"Ha, ha. Smart ass."

"You asked the question. We can watch them at my place. Okay?"

I nod in agreement. His place. I like the sound of that.

Once in Blockbuster, Jalen makes it known right off the bat that we will not be watching any love stories. I just look at him and roll my eyes.

"I saw that," he says, referring to me rolling my eyes.

"I wasn't trying to hide it," I respond.

"Okay, this is how we're going to do this. You pick a movie, and I'll pick a movie."

"You came up with that idea all by yourself?"

"Keep it up, Kaye. Keep it up."

We each head in opposite directions for our special pick.

I choose *Last Holiday* and find Jalen to let him know that I've made my selection. "Hey, I got mine," I say as I hand him the DVD.

"I thought I told you no love stories," he says a he points to the back of the DVD.

"Jalen, this isn't a love story. It's a story about a woman who thought she was going to die and decides to live life to the fullest."

"No love stories. I already know that the only reason you picked that up is because LL is in it."

"You just can't take competition, can you?" I say as a chuckle.

"No competition there. No love stories. Choose something else," he responds to my comment.

I put the movie back and continue on my quest for a movie. I look around the new titles and they all seem to be based on some sort of love story. I end up choosing *Rent*, which is actually a musical. I look around for Jalen, and I see he's standing at the counter looking around, no doubt, for me.

As I get closer to him, I see that he has chosen *War of the Worlds*. He looks in my hand and sees the selection I've made and shakes his head.

"You said no love stories. This is a musical."

"Girl, if you don't choose something else, we're going to be watching ESPN all night."

"Okay. Give me a minute," I say as I head back to look for another movie. I search and search. I really don't see anything that I just have to see. I eventually just pick an action film.

Jalen just stares at me as I walk toward him. He looks in my hand and sees that I've chosen *Munich*.

"Will this do?" I say as I wave the movie tirelessly in the air.

"Bring it," he replies.

Jalen pays for the movies and we make our way toward his place to continue our date.

Oops, I Did it Again

We pull up to Jalen's house—I mean his mansion. It is immaculate. He hits the garage button, and we pull in.

"Do you live here by yourself?" I ask.

"Of course not. I have four hundred women who frequent the palace."

"Somehow, Jalen, I don't take that as a joke."

"Lighten up, baby girl."

He opens the door, and his interior is just as fabulous as the exterior— vaulted ceilings, terra cotta walls, African-American art, and furniture in bold colors.

"Before you ask, I didn't decorate. My mom did."

"It's beautiful, Jalen."

"Thanks."

"Let's go to the theater."

"The theater? You have a theater room?"

"Yeah. It's a little perk."

Why don't I ever get little perks? I think.

The theater room is really nice. It is decorated in

browns and blacks. There is seating for eight with a wrap-around sofa in the back. Very relaxing.

"So, Miss Lady, what do you want to watch first?"

I point to *War of the Worlds*, and he puts it in. I sit in one of the LaZ Boy chairs. It immediately begins to vibrate. I jump. Jalen starts laughing.

"Jalen, that's not funny."

"No, but your reaction was."

I can't help but laugh. I'm uptight about some things. I try to relax.

"Thirsty?"

"No, I'm fine. Thanks," I say, a little apprehensive at the fact that he practically laughs at everything that I do.

"Let's sit on the sofa. It's more comfortable."

I join him on the sofa as we begin to watch the movie. He moves closer to me. I can feel the heat escaping his body. I don't know why I tense up. We're already passed the shy stage. He puts his arm around me, and I almost faint. Could he really want me? It seems unfathomable, but I'm here in his house, in his arms. What's so unbelievable about that?

I'm not sure when Jalen starts kissing me. I'm not even sure when he penetrates me. All I know is that I'm lying on his bed totally succumbing to his actions. Am I dreaming? Have to be. I open my eyes, and nope it's not a dream because he's turned me over, and he's exploring my body from that position that is so familiar to dogs.

"Jalen," I whisper.

He doesn't respond.

"Jalen."

"Yes, baby?"

I say nothing as the next sound I hear is me gasping in excitement, squealing and screaming, trying not to faint because he is rendering me temporarily unstable. Suddenly, my emotions are all over the place, and I'm too excited. We dance and dance. Our silhouettes are bouncing all over the walls. We climax, and our bodies fall together but separately.

He kisses me. I kiss him back. The dance we just performed must have been the dress rehearsal. The real show is just getting started. When we finish our final scene, our bodies are drenched in sweat, and we're too weak to move. We lay, just looking into each other's eyes, exploring the possibilities of what's to come.

"Kaye, what are you doing to me?"

"Jalen, I'm not doing anything to you. I feel like I'm the one in a trance."

He raises up and heads to the bathroom. I just lie still. Then it hits me. Where's the condom? I search in the covers and on the floor. Nothing. That's what he went to the bathroom for, I decide. He calls me back into the bathroom. I think before I move, not sure if my legs can support the rest of my body. I walk into the bathroom and smile at the sight before me. Jalen has filled the Jacuzzi tub and lit candles. How romantic. My doubts are temporarily laid to rest. He definitely likes me as he guides me into the tub after him and relaxes me on his chest. It can't get any better than this.

"Jalen," I say as the music comes on, and Luther is crooning about nothing better than love," how do you really feel about me?" I ask.

"I'm into you, Kaye. If I wasn't, trust me, I would have never allowed you to enter my home or my bed."

"Then why is it so hard for you to be with me exclusively?"

"I told you. I'm not ready. Just chill and let this thing grow on me. We don't have to rush into anything right now, okay?"

"Okay," I say in agreement, but not really agreeing.

I lay my head back and listen to Tamia and Fabolous talk about being so into each other.

When I awake, I find myself back in Jalen's bed. How does he do that? I must have fell asleep. I didn't even feel him move me. I turn, and he's fast asleep. I kiss him on his back and pull him closer to me. I guess it's too late to turn back now because I'm in love. I find myself getting sleepy again, but before I can close my eyes, I hear music. It's not the radio. The sound is sweet but somber. Sounds familiar. Sounds like that damn theme from *Titanic* again. Who in the hell keeps playing that damn music?

You Got It Bad

Yesterday was wonderful. I'm just glad I don't have to go to work today because I would have never made it. After spending the night with Jalen, I need to return home, so I catch a cab while he is still sleeping.

It's twelve o'clock now, and I check my messages. I have ten, and they're all from Tori. I return her call.

"Where have you been, fast heifer? I've been looking for you all night. I thought somebody had molested you. Are you just getting in? Where the hell have you been?"

"Good afternoon, Tori. It's great to hear from you."

"Bitch, don't start."

"Hey, let's just do something. You, Nyla, and me—a girl day—before I have to return to work tomorrow."

"Okay. Let's go shopping. Nyla needs some new shoes."

"Does Nyla need new shoes or do you want some new shoes?"

"Nyla, Tori. Same thing."

"Girl, you are hilarious. Where's Dre?"

"He just left to go to Jalen's discuss contracts and legal stuff, so can you have us for the rest of the day. I haven't forgotten you haven't told me about what happened at the club with Jalen."

"I'll tell you. Hey, Tori?"

"What?"

"Can we just stay at your place and watch movies and eat pizza?"

"Sure. What's up, Kaye?"

"I'll tell you when I get there."

"Okay."

"See ya in a little bit."

When I get to Tori's home, she and Nyla are on the floor playing with blocks in the den. She's already ordered the pizza, and the movie is playing. She always starts without me.

"Hey, girl," I say.

"What's up, Kaye? Something's wrong."

"No," I reply as I grab Nyla and sit on the floor across from Tori. I just missed you all, that's it."

"Kaye? Never mind. If you want to be stubborn, whatever, so what happened with you and Jalen?"

I look across the room so she can't see my eyes. I know if she looks into my eyes she will know.

"Oh my God, you didn't. Kaye, tell me you didn't."

I look at her with tears in my eyes. "I didn't mean

for it to happen. It just did. Besides you told me too."

"I didn't think you would actually do it. I should not have left you alone with him. How did it happen?"

"When we left the club, we both were still hyped. We started dancing, and one thing led to the next."

"Did you want to?"

"I did, but I was scared and nervous, and he was so sexy, and my mind was telling me one thing, and my body was saying another."

"So, you gave him some?"

"Yep."

"Was it good?"

I look at her and smile.

"Yep. It was good. You're glowing, girl. So where's the dust rag?"

"What dust rag?"

"The one he used to knock the dust off that—"

"Tori! I can't believe you just said that."

"You know it's true."

"But you didn't have to say that."

"So, what was it like?"

"Girl, I can't believe it happened. It was like my body was there but I was in a trance."

"He got you good, didn't he?"

"Yes. And Tori?" She looks at me intently. "We did it twice last night."

"You nasty heifer. I knew it."

"He took me to his house, and girl, we did it in the theater room and then his bedroom. I loved it. I think

I love him."

"Does Jalen know that? You know Jalen's a player, and the women flock to him. Do you think he's ready for a commitment?"

"First of all, I didn't tell him. He told me he wasn't ready for a commitment. He said he wanted to spend time with me. He took me out to eat last night. We had a great time. I know he likes me. I can see it in his eyes."

"Oh really? You know men. He's probably just feeling you out."

"I hope so."

"So, is it true?"

"What?"

"Does he use magnum condoms?"

I look at her and quickly bow my head in shame. Her question is a reminder of how careless we were.

"Oh Kaye, do tell."

"What?" I question.

"Tell me you didn't screw him without a condom. How could you be so negligent? You don't know how many other women he's getting down with. That wasn't smart. Not smart at all."

"I know. I know. He said that it was okay. I stopped him, but he didn't have anything on him, and you already know my story. I feel bad enough without you blazing me."

"I'm sorry. I know it's not like you to be so irresponsible."

"You told me to enjoy myself."

"I didn't tell you to be a risk taker."

I pick up Nyla and walk to the kitchen to get a soda. I have to get away from Tori. Nyla playfully grabs my hair and takes it to her mouth. I pull her hand away and she coos. She is so adorable.

Suddenly, the phone rings. Tori gets up to answer it as I continue to play with Nyla.

"Hey, Kaye," Tori yells, "your freak of the week is on the phone."

I run to the den, trying to make sure Jalen doesn't hear. I answer the phone with Nyla in tow.

"Hi, Jalen."

"Hey, baby girl."

"What's up?"

"I called you at your crib and you weren't there, so I figured you were hanging out with the ice princess."

"She's not like that, Jalen."

"Yeah, right. But check this out."

"I'm listening."

"I'm going away for a while—you know training camp—and I wanted to tell you that I'll be busy so you wouldn't think I ran out on you or anything."

"Alright," I say, puzzled as to if we are just friends why he would call to tell me this.

"So, I'll call you when things start to settle down, and maybe you can take off work and come to some games this season."

"I'd like that a lot, Jalen," I say with delight.

"I guess I'll holla then."

"Yeah. Okay. Bye."

I look at Tori, and she's smiling ear to ear. "Girl, you got it bad. What did he say?"

"He wanted me to know he was going to training camp and he'll call me later when he's free."

"Great. Kaylondria's got a man at home," she sings.

"You are so silly. I miss him already. How long is the season?"

She looks at me and shakes her head.

It's a good thing that I have a demanding job. It'll make the time that Jalen is away go by faster.

After the movie, I prepare to leave. "Well, girl, it's been quite nice but some of us have to work," I say coyly as I hand Nyla back to Tori but not before I kiss her little hand. "Take care of my goddaughter. I'll call you tomorrow. And Tori," I say as I see Dre pulling up, "don't do anything I wouldn't."

"Nasty, nasty," she yells.

She doesn't know how long I've wanted to tell her that.

As I'm walking out, Dre's walking in. I gave him a big hug.

"What's up, baby girl?"

"Nothing. Just visiting my friend."

"Seems like somebody's in a real good mood. I guess I don't even need to ask why."

"What did Jalen tell you?"

"Oh nothing," he says as he winks repeatedly.

Men. I believe they're worse than women. They gossip just like if not more than we do. I'm going to kill Jalen when I see him for putting my business out in the street.

I walk in the office, and the atmosphere seems quite dull. Maybe I've been away too long. I speak to my assistant, and she gives me a half smile.

"What's up, Tina?"

"Kaye, some things have changed."

"What things?"

"I don't think it's my place to tell you."

"Just tell me okay, Tina?"

Before she gets a chance, my boss, William Turner, informs me that he would like to see me in the conference room. I look at Tina quizzically, and she just bows her head. I wonder what the hell is going on.

As I walk in the conference room, I see all the bigwigs sitting and communing lightly. Not a good sign. Something is definitely going down.

"Good morning," I say half heartedly.

"Good morning," they all say in unison.

"Miss Parker, please join us," William says as he extends a hand to a seat directly in front of him. Reluctantly, I sit down.

"Miss Parker, how was your vacation?" he asks in an unconcerned tone.

Why is he being so formal? "It was wonderful, Mr. Turner," I respond, keeping with the formalities.

"Good. You're a hard worker, and you deserve some time off."

"Thanks," I reply.

"Miss Parker—" Here he goes again. I shift in my chair and look at all the faces around me. "I guess you're wondering why you're here."

I simply nod.

"The fact of the matter is we have some bad news. The company has been bought in a merger."

"What does that mean?" I ask in total panic.

"It means that we have to downsize."

"Who bought us?"

"Simon Industries," William replies. "They're on the move, and we didn't want to miss the chance for advancement in a better market. They're expanding the production and marketing department."

"Great. So that means more business and more opportunities to prosper."

"Well in a way—"

"Great. I have some ideas that could help us become more visible in the scientific field."

"That's why I love you. You're always creating."

"Thanks," I say in sheer delight.

He looks at me and scratches his temple.

"Miss Parker, unfortunately they're bringing their own people in, and we have to let you go."

"Let me go where? What are you saying?"

"Miss Parker, your services are no longer needed."

As soon as I open my mouth, Mr. Goldman, the

CFO interjects, "Don't fear, Miss Parker. We plan to give you a nice severance package that will compensate you for the services and dedication you have brought this company."

"But…you're firing me?"

"We're sorry there was no other way," William says as he looks at me with pity.

I sit in silence as everyone begins to clear the boardroom. How can I be fired? I take my first vacation in three years, and this is what I get? I can't believe it. I start to tremble. How am I going to survive? I watch as everybody starts walking out of the conference room like what just happened meant nothing.

"Kaye, are you alright?" William asks.

"You knew and you didn't call me? How could you?"

"I fought hard for you, Kaye. They just wanted to keep their people. They were adamant about it. It just so happened that a large majority of lab workers were able to keep their jobs."

"So what was I, the sacrificial lamb?"

"Kaye, don't do that."

"Do what?"

"Turn this into a sexual, racial thing."

"That's easy for you to say. You still have a job. What am I going to do?"

"You'll be fine. I'll make sure the package is enough for you to live on for a while."

"I can't believe this," I say as the tears begin to fall

uncontrollably.

"Look, Kaye, I'll keep my ears open, and if I hear something, I'll let you know."

"Yeah." I smirk. "Just like you let me know that I was being ousted from a company that I helped to build."

I get up and grab my purse. When I finally make it to my office, I am mentally exhausted. I have to walk down the hall with my head up when all I want to do was cry.

Tina comes in and asks me if I am okay. I tell her I'm fine. I just need a box. I sit in my chair and lay my head on my desk. I only lift it to acknowledge the knock on the door. It is Tina returning with a box.

She hands it to me in silence. I nod. She leaves. Just like that, years of hard work and sacrifice end with me once again holding the short end of the stick. I wonder why it seems as if I'm always getting screwed. It's a good thing I've been saving money. I'll need every dime to keep my head above water.

I gather my belongings, and I turn to go into William's office and hand him my key pass.

He starts talking about how it was a pleasure working with me and he wishes me…That's all I hear because I walk out the door. He doesn't respect me enough to let me know about a merger that I am sure didn't take place over the course of a weekend, so why would I respect him enough to listen to his falsities? I don't even tell Tina good-bye. People start calling my name from all directions. I ignore them all as the elevator opens and I step in with my back to them. What more can I do? It's already full of knives. I heave once and the door closes. I cry so hard it hurts. I threw everything into my career. I don't know what else to do.

I must have driven the whole way home on autopilot 'cause all I know is that I made my way to my apartment in one piece. I quickly head up the stairs and run the shower. I must stay in it for a while because the water becomes cold.

I get dressed and head to my bed. I notice the message light on my answering machine is blinking. I push the button to retrieve my messages. I'm informed that I have four new ones. The first is from Mrs. Andrews of my church. She's calling to remind me to bring a dish for the picnic for Saturday afternoon. The next three are from Tori babbling about some sale. No Jalen. Sounds about right. My life sucks.

I go to the bathroom to look for something to take for this massive headache that I have. I find some Motrin and take three from the bottle. I also grab three Benadryl to help me sleep. I need to just go to sleep and maybe when I wake up things will be different.

I awaken only to hear Tori screaming and yelling. "What? What?" I say still groggy.

"Heifer, it's eight o'clock."

"What are you doing up so early?" I question.

"It's night time," she screams at the top of her lungs.

"Well, that means I've only been asleep for a few hours."

"Kaye, it's Wednesday."

"Wednesday? I slept for a whole day."

"Yes, ma'am. I've been calling you like crazy. When I got no answer, I was worried so I came over. What did you do?"

"I just took some Motrin and Benadryl."

"You've missed work."

No. No. No. No. It came back to like a ton of bricks. "I was fired."

"What?"

"I mean let go. I mean fired. Shit, it's all the same." I find myself crying all over again as I unfold the news to Tori. She is agitated but still supportive.

"It's okay. If you need anything, just ask."

"Okay, but they promised me compensation. It's a good thing it's just me. I'll survive. I should be okay for a couple of months."

"Kaye, I'm so sorry. I know how much you love your job."

"Thanks. I guess it wouldn't have hurt so much if I saw it coming."

"Well, there is good news."

"Oh yeah. What? You just saved a fortune on your

car insurance?"

She just looks at me and shakes her head. "Now you can hang out with me all day."

I scream sarcastically, "Yes!"

"Watch it, you broke chick."

I look at her and roll my eyes.

"You'll be fine. You'll see."

I exhale. I know she's right. I've been through more and made it through. This is only a roadblock.

Why Ask Why?

It's been two months since I've heard from Jalen. I'm starting to think it was all for naught. It's cool though because I'm keeping Nyla for a week until Dre and Tori come back from vacation. We're having a blast. They will be back tomorrow. My dog, Coco's actually enjoying Nyla. Coco seems to think Nyla is a toy.

As I put Nyla on the sofa, I get a cramp in my stomach. I go into the bathroom and check the calendar and it is definitely that time of the month. I am so stressed I didn't even get my period last month. I'm glad that it's coming.

I go to the kitchen and make me some warm tea and pop some popcorn. I watch what seems like movie after movie. Around nine-thirty, the phone rings. I answer it and light up when I hear the voice at the other end. It's Jalen.

"Hey, baby girl."

"Hey, Jalen. What's up?"

"Nothing. Just trying to holla back. I miss you."

I smile with delight. "I miss you too."

"What have you been up to?"

"I'm babysitting my goddaughter."

"That's cool."

"Tori and Dre are on vacation. They'll be back tomorrow. How's the season going?"

"It's going pretty good. We haven't lost a game yet."

"That's terrific."

"It's been great. The training is paying off. I was wondering though…I got some tickets, and I know Dre and Tori are coming, do you wanna come to a game?"

"Sure. I would love it."

"Okay. I gotta go. I'll holla back."

"Bye," I say as I hang up the phone in sheer excitement. I'm getting butterflies in my stomach. I can't believe he actually called me. I can't wait until Tori comes back. We need to go shopping. I know I'm on a budget but I'm going to make sure I represent at the game.

I wake up this morning to Nyla's screams. I have a terrible pounding headache, and I feel hot. I must have a temperature. I try to pacify Nyla, but she's not buying it. We do this for the next five hours. She must really miss her parents.

By two o'clock, I am drenched in sweat. I've taken a shower twice, and I'm still burning up. I decide to call Tori.

"Hey, Tori."

"Hey, girl. The nanny-sitting is getting old and you're ready for us to come home, aren't you? Well, we'll be there in about an hour."

"No, it's not that. I must have some twenty-four-hour bug. I have a pounding headache, and I'm burning up."

"Okay. Can you hold on until we get there and I'll take you to the emergency room?"

"Sure. I can wait." And I do. It seems like the clock goes backward before it goes forward. Nyla finally decides to take a nap, and I'm glad. I've bathed and fed her and she's still upset. I feel as if I'm losing my mind. I go to the bathroom and look in the mirror. My skin is turning pale. What the hell's wrong with me? I've never felt like this before.

I must've passed out because when I come to, I'm in an emergency room hooked up to an I.V. I look to my right, and I see Tori holding my hand. She looks hella worried. I squeeze her hand to let her know that I'm okay.

"Hey, precious," she states in a motherly tone I rarely see.

"Hey," I reply in a weak voice.

"Are you feeling better?"

"I feel a lot better. How did I get here?"

"You were passed out on the floor when we made it, so Dre put you in your car, and I rushed you here.

He took Nyla home."

"Thanks," I say in tears.

"Why are you crying?"

"I don't know what I would do without you. What about Nyla? Is she okay? I didn't mean to leave her unattended."

"She's fine. She was still sleeping when we made it there."

"I'm so sorry."

"What are you apologizing for? You didn't know you were that sick. It's okay and—"

Before she can finish the sentence, the doctor walks in.

"How are you feeling, Miss Parker?"

"I'm okay. I just feel groggy and a little tired."

"It's the medicine wearing off. The good news is that we're going to release you today. We think you'll be fine. You suffered from what seems to be a stress attack, but it was heightened by your condition. If you watch your stress levels, you'll be fine."

I see Tori furrowing her eyebrows, and I'm looking at the doctor totally confused. Am I dying? What condition is he referring to? Before I can verbalize my thoughts, Tori does it for me.

"What condition?"

"You don't know?" the doctor asks as he looks from Tori to me suspiciously.

"No," I say in a childlike tone.

"You're pregnant."

"Pregnant," Tori and I both exclaim at the same time.

"Yes. Congratulations," the doctor says, grinning from ear to ear. "I'll go now to prepare your release papers."

All of a sudden, I feel myself getting sicker. I turn away from Tori because I can't bear to see her expression. We sit in total silence until the nurse returns and unhooks the machines and removes the I.V. I get dressed and head to the checkout counter and sign the release papers. The nurse hands me some prescriptions.

Tori and I ride all the way back to my apartment in total silence. Tori turns back my bed and puts me under the covers.

"You get some rest. I'll go to the pharmacy to pick up your medicine."

The doctor had prescribed me some prenatal vitamins along with some pain pills for my headache.

"Okay," I reply weakly and in total shock. I can't believe this is happening to me. I must be a magnet for bad luck. As I hear her close the bedroom door, I burst into tears. What am I going to do with a baby? I'll probably be homeless in nine months. But most importantly, how am I going to tell Jalen?

It's now eleven in the morning as I look at the clock. As I enter the living room, I see Tori and Nyla on the floor playing with blocks. I look at them in awe.

I could never be a mother. Not a good one anyway. I wonder what my baby will be like. Will it be a boy or a girl? Will it look like me or Jalen? Jalen. Damn. I have to tell him. I don't know how, but I'll have to muster up enough courage to talk to him.

Tori sees me, and she smiles. I exhale. It's time to talk.

"Are you feeling better?" she asks

"Yeah. Thanks, Tori, for everything. I know you wanna go home. I'll be okay."

"I'm fine. I'm gonna bunk with you tonight. I wanna be certain you're okay."

"Thanks," I say as I sit next to her.

"What are you going to do, Kaye?"

"I don't know. I guess I need to talk to Jalen first. I'm not sure how receptive he'll be to the news."

"He'll get over it. It's a baby, not the plague."

"He called before I went into the hospital. He wants me to come to a game. He said you guys were going."

"Yeah, they're playing Tampa. Are you sure you're going to be okay to go?"

"The doctor said I'll be fine if I just watch my stress levels."

"Well the game is Sunday. You need to get plenty of rest before then."

"I know. Tori?"

"What?

"Do you think I'm stupid?"

"Hell no. I think that you were a woman who need- ed some comfort, and you found it. You're not the first person to get pregnant, and I'm sure you won't be the last. I just can't believe you had unprotected sex with Jalen. But why ask why."

"I know, but I feel hypnotized when he's around. All common sense goes out the window. What do you think his reaction will be?"

"He's a man. Who knows?"

"I just hope he'll be supportive. There's no way pos- sible I could raise a baby alone, especially now that I don't have a job."

Sunday is finally here. I've been sick all morning. I thought about not going to the game but Jalen's already expecting me. Expecting. That's funny. I hear the horn that signals Dre and Tori are outside. I grab my purse and keys and head out the door, but not before saying bye to Coco.

I get into the Escalade, and Dre automatically turns to me and says "What's up?" I give him a com- plimentary nod. Tori's quiet. That's unusual. She must be nervous.

"Hey, y'all," I say nonchalantly.

Tori asks me how I'm feeling without looking directly at me.

"Better" is all I can say.

As we park at the stadium, we see Jalen outside talking to some chick who looks like she came straight out of *Elle* magazine. If you ask me, she's a little over-dressed for a football game. I don't know what she's saying, but Jalen is smiling from ear to ear. Go figure.

We walk toward him, and he never even notices us. Dre intervenes, "What up, dog?"

"What's up, my boy?" Jalen responds.

He looks at me awkwardly. I turn to look at the walking Barbie. He introduces us.

"Andrea, I would like you to meet my friends, Dre, Tori, and Kaye. Everybody, this is Andrea."

We all nod but no words are spoken.

"I'll meet up with you later, Jalen," she says, stroking his hand and obviously his ego as he rubs his chin.

"What's up, baby girl?" he says as he reaches out and hugs me.

"What's up, Jalen?" I say in an agitated voice.

"Ain't nothing, just chillin'. How about a pregame meal?"

"Sure," we all say.

The team restaurant is so beautiful. The ambience is a mixture of a restaurant and a bar. Looking at all the food and the lights makes me feel queasy all over again.

"What's wrong, baby girl? Your salad isn't fresh?" Jalen asks me after he notices that I'm just playing with my food.

"No. I'm just not real hungry." I feel the odors tugging at my insides. "Excuse me," I say as I rush to the restroom.

Once in the bathroom, I let go of what seems like everything I've eaten in the past two days. I don't know if I can go through six and a half more months of this. I turn to see Tori handing me a pack of saltines.

"Thanks."

"You're welcome. You're going to have to keep some of these in your purse."

"Will this morning sickness last forever?"

"It shouldn't, but you need to be prepared."

"Does Dre know?"

"Yes. He was questioning me so much I had to tell him the truth. I couldn't lie to him."

"I would expect nothing less. What did he have to say about it?"

"Nothing really. He just wanted to know what you were planning on doing."

"I don't know. What do you think?"

"I think you and Jalen need to talk about it, but not until after the game."

"I can't believe I have something growing inside me."

"Yep. The joys of pregnancy. And guess what?"

"What?"

"I'm going to be an auntie. I'm going to be an auntie," she says, excited.

"Tori, I'm scared."

"Of course you are, and you damn well should be. This shit ain't easy."

"Thanks a lot, Tori. That really makes me feel a whole lot better about the situation."

"I'm just giving it to you straight. Your belly swells, your face swells, your breasts swell, and your feet swells. Hell, you're going to be walking around like a balloon. That's why I refuse to do it again, no matter what Dre says. I'm popping birth control pills left and right. Not happening."

"Does he know you're taking birth control pills?"

"Naw. He thinks we're just having a hard time. I keep telling him stuff like my cycle changes so much."

"He buys that?"

"None the wiser. Let's go back before they start suspecting something's up."

As we walk back to our table, I see Jalen and Dre talking furiously. They must be talking about football. They spot us and Dre looks up smiling. Jalen turns his head towards me and smiles also. I smile back.

"Is everything okay?" Jalen asks.

"Sure," Tori responds as she sits down next to Dre and finishes her meal.

I sit next to Jalen and listen to him and Dre finish their conversation. For the next fifteen minutes they talk about football, football, and more football. I become anxious and begin to move constantly.

"Ready to go, ladies?" Dre asks.

"Yeah, Dre," Tori responds.

Jalen places his hand in the small of my back, and I begin to get queasy once again.

"Well, I hate to mingle and run, but I've got some ass to kick out on the field. See ya after the game."

"Okay," I say as he kisses me on my forehead. He heads toward the locker room, and we head in the opposite direction toward our seats in the stadium.

I'm so glad the game is over. My whole body is aching. Tori, Dre, and I head downstairs to meet Jalen in the locker room.

"Jalen played a hell of a game, didn't he, ladies?" Dre asks.

"Yeah," we both say in unison, unaffected, obviously worn out from the day's festivities.

Dre heads into the locker room, and just before he enters, he yells, "Be out shortly."

"Girl, when are you going to tell Jalen?" Tori asks.

"I don't know, Tori. I'm not sure he's ready for this."

"Oh hell, he was definitely ready for it," she says adamantly.

"What if he says it's not his?"

"Of course he'll say that. He's a man. You have to make him understand that—"

Before she could say another word, Dre and Jalen appear, beaming.

"Congratulations," I say nervously, although I meant it literally.

"Thanks, ma," Jalen says, grinning like a little boy.

"Yo, man, that game was hot," Dre exclaims.

"Man, it was hard. They put up a hell of a fight."

Tori looks at Jalen quizzically and responds with "Obviously not," referring to the 27–7 score.

"I do believe it's time for a celebration. Just let me do a few interviews with the media, and I'll be right back," Jalen says.

We wait for what seems like an hour before Jalen appears again. He is too ecstatic.

"Okay, ladies and gent, let's head to the club. It's time to party."

I look at Tori. She nods, which only means I'm going to the club.

Dre and Jalen talk the entire way. Tori and I sit quietly as she holds my hand. She's right. I guess I'm going to have to tell him at some point. I might as well do it while he's in a good mood.

As soon as we enter the VIP, girls are screaming Jalen's name. I feel like a fish out of water. But surprisingly, Jalen doesn't pay them any mind. Maybe he does care a little bit about me.

"Hey," I say, rubbing his back and·interrupting a conversation with a few of his teammates.

"What's up, baby girl?"

"Nothing. Just wanted to give you a hug."

He replies by pulling me so close I feel as if I'm his second skin.

Drinks come around, and he pushes a Long Island Iced Tea into my hands. "Jalen, you know I don't drink."

"Yeah, but I thought we already had this conversation about you loosening up. Drink."

"But, Jalen, I can't."

"You can and you will. Come on, baby. It's my party. Celebrate with me."

I nod because I don't want to disappoint him. As I lift the glass to my lips, Tori swings around from nowhere and spills the drink on the floor—a bona fide pro. I'm relieved. She glares at me and starts walking toward a private VIP room. I follow suit.

"What the hell are you doing?"

"Jalen kept insisting that I drink."

"Girl, you gonna have a two-headed baby. You need to tell him."

"Okay. Okay. Tonight."

Walking back out to the floor, I see this wench trying to steer Jalen to the dance floor. She's rubbing on his chest and whispering in his ear. I start feeling sick to my stomach. I spin to go use the restroom, and I feel a hand clinching my waist. When I turn around, it's Jalen pulling me to the dance floor. "Cater 2 U" is blasting through the speakers. Great, I need to throw up and he wants to dance.

He pulls me so that my back is to his chest. We're swaying, and he's grinding with his hands holding my arms. He places his left hand on my stomach, and I tense up. I wonder if he can tell. I start to feel dizzy. I don't know if it's from the smoke or the stench or Jalen's gesture, but I need some fresh air.

I pull away and run to the bathroom. Luckily, no one is there. I expell the contents I didn't even know I had. I must be in here for a while because Jalen sends Tori after me.

"Girl, we have to get you home now."

"What did he say? Did he asks you questions?"

"Naw. He just told me you ran off."

"Oh my God, Tori."

"What?"

"He rubbed my stomach, and I was so queasy...I had to leave."

"Too much anxiety. Let's blow this joint."

She spots a girl whispering in Dre's ear.

"This nasty-ass heifer has been chasing my man all night. If I stay here another minute, I'm going to have to kick her ass."

"Let's go," I say hurriedly. Tori can be straight hood when she wants to.

When we get to the exit, Jalen and Dre appear.

"You alright?" Jalen asks, all concerned.

"Yes, Jalen. All this smoke and funk is getting to me."

"Alright let's go." Everybody nods in agreement. I'm so glad.

The ride back to the football stadium is pretty much the same as the ride to the club. When we pull in the parking lot, Tori and Dre hop out. I get out with them since they brought me. Tori flashs me one of her deadly looks, and I sit my happy self right back down.

"Oh, Jalen," Tori says coolly, "can you please see to it that Kaye gets home safely?"

"You bet."

And with that I hop in the front seat, and Jalen and I are alone. "So, baby girl, did you enjoy the game?"

"Yeah, it was exciting," I lie.

"It's late and I'm exhausted. Why don't you stay at my house so we don't have to make a trip across town?"

"Okay," I reply. Now is the perfect time to tell him.

When we make it to Jalen's, I head into the great room.

"Yo, baby girl?" Jalen calls.

"Um-huh," I reply.

"Let's take a bath. Are you hungry? Thirsty?"

"No, Jalen, I'm fine, but I don't have any clothes to sleep in."

"Don't worry. You won't need any."

What the hell? I say to myself.

As we're soaking in the hot tub listening to jazz, he kisses me on my neck.

"Kaye, I've really been enjoying your company. Things have changed a lot since the night we spent together. I know I haven't been spending as much time with you as you would like. It's been hectic preparing for the season and everything. I promise that as soon as the season is over, I'll be able to donate more time to you. Maybe we can do something for the holidays."

"I understand, Jalen. So much has happened over the last few months. It's been like a whirlwind," I whisper.

"I know."

"Have your feelings about me changed at all?" I ask, trying to pry information out of him that will help me disclose my pregnancy to him better.

"Kaye, you're special to me, not like all the other girls who be running after me just so they can get to my bank account. I'm not looking for a relationship. I already told you that I love spending time with you."

"Me too," I reply, brokenhearted. How can I tell him that our weekend of lust has created another living soul? He clearly doesn't want to be with me.

He yanks me out of the tub, interrupting my train of thought. He lays me on the bed and climbs on top of me. I can't let him do this until he knows. I've gotta say something, but before I can make my mouth move to utter any words, I feel Jalen inside me. His lovemaking is tantalizing. When I'm with him, my mind seems to drift to another place—a place where there's serenity and calmness. Then it hits me. That's exactly how I got in this predicament in the first place.

Jalen is sound asleep while I lay awake pondering ways to tell him about the baby. It's already six o'clock in the morning, and I don't think I've gotten an hour of sleep. I might as well get up. I head to the bathroom and find an extra toothbrush. While I'm brushing, Jalen sneaks up and scares the hell out of me.

"Jalen," I shout in fright, "you almost scared me to

death."

"Sorry. I couldn't resist. Babygirl, you look tired. I didn't think I wore you out that bad."

"Yeah. Whatever."

"Anyway, Siedah has prepared breakfast for us. I can't believe you get up with the roosters."

I smile devilishly.

Mounting the stairway, I can smell the aroma of hickory bacon, sausage, eggs, pancakes, and something sweet. It's amazing how now that I'm pregnant my sense of smell is better than a bloodhound. I don't know who this Siedah chick is, but she definitely deserves a raise.

Jalen has breakfast set out on the patio. I greet Siedah who's an elderly black woman and thank her graciously for breakfast.

"See you found something to wear." Jalen points to me, referring to his Sean John shirt.

"Yeah, I needed something that would allow me to feel free," I say as we head towards the kitchen.

I look down at my watch and it reads six-thirty. I want to go to service. So, I decide to mention this to Jalen.

"I'm used to going to eight o'clock service, Jalen."

"You better catch it via TV because after I eat, I'm going back to bed."

"Jalen!"

"What? I'm serious. I only get up this early because Siedah always fixes Sunday breakfast around six. I eat and then I return to bed."

"Why don't you attend services?" I ask him curiously.

"I do. I just don't go at eight o'clock."

"Jalen?" I ask him.

He furrows his eyebrows. "What?"

"Why are you getting antsy with me?"

"I'm not. You've been calling my name for the last eight hours."

I respond by throwing a piece of bacon at him, which he catches and eats. "Waste not, want not."

"Sure."

"If you really want to go to church," he rambles as he looks at his watch, "nah, not gonna make it. It's already seven-thirty. I tell you what, if you wait, we can go to night service. Okay?"

"Okay. Whatever you say. Jalen, do you trust me?"

"Trust you to do what?"

"Just trust me period."

"I…umm…I" He looks at me. "I…really don't trust anyone, babygirl. What's up?"

I see I'm going to have to try a different approach. "I lost my job," I blurt out before I realize what I'm saying.

"When?" he asks, jumping up from the table.

"Two and half months ago."

"What happened?"

"The company upgraded, and they didn't need me anymore."

"So, how are you getting by?"

"Savings and my severance package."

"Why are you just telling me this now?"

"Because you've been busy and it was my problem. I didn't want to bother you."

"Damn, Kaye. That's fucked up."

"I know. I invested a lot of time and energy doing research for that company."

"So, what are you going to do?"

"Look for another job before I have to start swinging on a pole."

He smiles. "I like that thought. I know just the right club. Girl, you can be a millionaire by the end of the year—that's after my fifty percent cut."

"Jalen, that's cruel."

"Hey, I got a mortgage too."

"Ha, ha. Ha, ha," I say sarcastically.

"Laugh if you wanna. Let's see how many more free meals you'll be eating over here."

I look at him sideways. Somehow I don't think he means that as a joke.

We finish breakfast and go back upstairs. With each step, I begin to feel more and more nauseated. My head is spinning. I can't see straight. I try to reach and call for Jalen, but nothing comes out of my mouth. The room seems to be rotating at a high speed, and before I can focus, I pass out.

It's All Out in the Open

When I come to, I see I am hooked up to machines. This seems like déjá vu. It has to be. Damn. I'm in the hospital again. *Lord, please let Tori have brought me. I'm begging you,* I pray. When I look up, in walks Jalen.

"Hey," I say.

Nothing. Damn he already knows. The nurses come in and begin to check my pressure and my heart rate. Jalen is refusing to look at me. He does know. He glances at the nurse and nods, but quickly averts his eyes from me. I reach for the phone. I need to call Tori. I dial the numbers, and all the while Jalen has his back to me. Tori's not answering. I turn on my side and start weeping.

We must have sat in that room for hours because when I look at the clock it reads five-thirty. Jalen's angry. He refuses to look up at me. Somebody has to say something, so I guess it will have to be me.

"Jalen, could you call Tori for me, please?"

"She's out of town. Went to visit her mother," he says as he paces around the room.

"Oh. I forgot," I reply disappointed. What am I going to do? I need Tori. Now.

"How long have you known?" he asks.

"How long have I known what?" I ask stupidly.

"Don't play with me, Kaye."

"About two months," I reply, not looking at him directly, picking an imaginary piece of lint from the blanket.

"And you didn't tell me because...?"

"I didn't know how."

"What in the hell are you talking about? I bet you told Tori."

"No, I didn't," I yell. "I passed out while keeping Nyla. She took me to the hospital. We both found out at the same time."

"Kaye, Kaye, Kaye, why?" he asks as he shakes his head in disgust.

"Why what?"

"Why did you choose me?"

"What the hell are you talking about? I didn't choose you for anything."

"This ain't about to go down like this."

"What? What are you talking about?"

"Look, we can't have a baby. It will mess up everything."

We are interrupted by the doctor who informs me

that I'm going to be discharged. He gives me a list of things to do to stay healthy. I nod for confirmation, and he tells me congratulations but not before Jalen walks out and slams the door. I guess it's all out in the open.

Jalen's been quiet since we left the hospital. Although he's doing the speed limit, I know he's pissed.

"Are you hungry?" he asks.

"A little," I reply.

"What do you want to eat?"

I open up the papers the doctor gave me and review the foods he says are healthy for the baby. I feel Jalen's stare upon me. I quickly toss the papers to the side and state, "Whatever you want, Jalen."

We pull up to this restaurant, and we hop out. Jalen leaves me. He's really pissed for sure. We sit down at a table in the corner, and when the waiter walks over Jalen places his order. I do the same.

"Jalen, please don't be mad."

"I'm not mad."

"You're not talking to me."

"I'm really not feeling this situation, Kaye."

"I told you that I wasn't on birth control. You insisted that we—"

"So, what now it's all my fault?" He bangs the table.

"No, I'm just saying, I didn't trick you or anything."

He looks at me, and for the first time, I notice

worry lines in the middle of his brows.

"Kaye, let me ask you the same question you asked me earlier. Do you trust me?"

I look into his eyes and state matter-of-factly, "Yes."

"Good. I know what we have to do. It'll be best. Now is not a good time. Taking care of a family is hard work. We can get it set up for tomorrow."

I can't believe my ears. He can't be asking me to do what I think he's saying. He states it like this isn't his first time. Before I can respond, the waiter returns with our food. But all of a sudden, I've completely lost my appetite.

Naturally, Jalen takes me home. I'm glad because I don't want to be around him any longer. Surprisingly, when I go upstairs, he follows.

"Thanks for bringing me home."

"You're not staying. Pack a bag and let's go. We got a long drive in the morning."

A long drive? Where in the hell is he taking me? I must have not been moving fast enough because he starts tossing items into my carry-on for me. I grab my dog and follow him. I need to talk to Tori. She'll know what to do. I dial her number but no answer. Damn. Guess I'm on my own.

I can hear Jalen running bathwater. He calls for me. Like a fool I run to him with Coco at my heels. He's already soaking in the tub. I join him.

He massages my shoulders. I think how could this be happening to me. What have I done to make life so hard for me? He strokes my hair. I flinch.

"Baby, it will be okay." I guess he's responding to my flinching when he touched me. "You'll see. Babies change everything. It'll be too hard."

"Your teammates have kids, and they're okay."

"Yeah, but they're in court a lot, and baby mamas be tripping over dollars and won't let them see their kids."

"I promise I won't ask you for child support, and you can see the baby whenever you like."

"So, what are you gonna feed and clothe it with, huh? Or have you forgotten that you don't have a job? I don't need you leeching off me."

"Jalen! I would never leech off you. My situation is only temporary."

"Yeah. Why would you go back to work if you had easy access to my money?"

I turn around in fury, causing water to spill onto the floor. "So that's what this is about? You don't want to be financially responsible for a child that you helped create? You are so fucking selfish, Jalen."

"Whatever. You're having the abortion tomorrow. You might as well prepare yourself for it."

I jump out the tub in a rage, dry off, and put on my yoga pants and a T-shirt and head outside to sit in the hammock with Coco.

How dare he? I think as I sway, crying uncontrollably. He doesn't love me. He doesn't respect me. He just wants me to be at his beck and call. I am not a maid servant. How do I continually place myself in these predicaments? I will never forgive him for making me do this.

I must have cried myself to sleep because when I wake up, Jalen is trying to get me to come inside. It is pretty cold. I jump out of the hammock with Coco under my arm and run inside of the house, but not before slamming the door in his face.

He is pissed when he comes upstairs. I'm in the middle of his bed sporting a tear-stained face. He starts to undress and slip into his night clothes. To hell with him. I don't give a damn if this is house. There ain't no way in hell he's sleeping in here with me. And with that thought in my mind, I begin tossing pillows at his trashy ass.

"What the hell's wrong with you?" he asks as he begins to pick up the pillows from the floor.

"Get the fuck out. Get the fuck out," I scream. "I hate you. Get out."

What shocks me the most is he does just that. I cry for what seems like forever. My heart is aching. I need to get a hold of Tori soon before I crash and burn completely, so I called her. *Please pick up. Please pick up. Please pick up.*

"Hello," she answers.

"Tori, it's me—Kaye. Please come get me now. I'm at Jalen's. I'll be waiting for you outside." I quickly hang up. Thank you, Jesus. Just what I need…a refuge.

It is freezing as I wait for Tori to pull up. I have to get out. I can't take a chance on Jalen knowing I'm leaving. He's sound asleep in the other bedroom as I tiptoe down the stairs and out of the kitchen patio. To hell with Jalen. If he doesn't want to be a father, fine. I'm keeping this baby no matter what. Come hell or high water. I can swim pretty well. It's the hell part that terrifies me.

As Tori pulls up, I don't even wait for the SUV to make a complete stop before I open the door and jump in.

"Hey, girl. What the hell has lit a fire under you?"

"Jalen. Just drive. I'll tell you later. Can we just go to a hotel?"

"Sure, but I need to tell Dre something."

"Can we just tell him you're staying at your mother's. I don't want Dre telling Jalen where we are."

Tori immediately calls Dre and tells him that she has to help her mother with something. She then looks at me and says, "Better."

"Good. Can we please keep it that way?" I plead. Then the floodgates open. I can't stop crying.

Tori is looking at me, worried. "Kaye? Kaye, what is it? Just tell me. What's going on?"

"It's all out in the open."

Foolish

I stay in the truck while Tori goes into the Marriott to get a room. I can't believe what is happening. I thought Jalen would be different. Why do I continue to play the fool? How could I be so stupid? What would actually make me think that I ever had a chance with a man like Jalen? The thought brings me back to my past, and I start crying all over again.

Tori approaches the truck and opens the door. She grabs my hand and walks me into the hotel. We ride the elevator in silence. It seems the weight of the world is resting on my shoulders. The weight is beginning to become unbearable. I need to find some relief from somewhere.

Tori sits me on the bed, grabs my bag and puts it on the chair. She sits next to me on the bed and rubs my back. I suddenly become overwhelmed, and before I know it, the tears seem to flow all on their own.

"What's wrong, Kaye? If you don't tell me, I can't

help you."

I look at her, and I lay my head on her shoulder and cry relentlessly. "How could he be so vicious?" is all I can say, shaking nervously.

"What happened? Tell me everything."

"I tried to call you. I passed out again at breakfast. He took me to the hospital. The doctor must have told him before I got a chance to. He was so upset, Tori," I say through tears. "He accused me of being dishonest and telling you before I told him. He said I was ruining everything. Tori, he scheduled an abortion for today. He said that a baby would allow me to have easy access to his bank account. How could he be so selfish? Why is he treating me like a one-night stand? How could I be so foolish?"

"Oh, sweetie, I'm so sorry. The audacity of him to just assume that an abortion is what you want."

"What am I going to do? All this stress can't be good for the baby."

"Kaye, what do you want?"

"Not to have to do this all by myself." I sigh wearily.

"Have you really told him that? Have you told him that you want to keep it?"

"No."

"Kaye, silence gives consent. You need to talk to him. You need to tell him how you feel or else he's going to make the decisions, whether you like it or not."

"His mind already seems to be made up."

"Yeah, but it's your job to help him understand. Not just for you, but also for this baby you're carrying. I see how good you are with Nyla. I know you'll make a wonderful mother."

"Thanks," I reply. I look out of the window of the sixth floor. Daydreaming. Envisioning what it will be like to be a mother. What if this is my only chance? I have to do something. I look at Tori who is obviously exhausted. Within minutes, she sprawls across the bed in a deep sleep. I know what I have to do now. In the morning, I'll face Jalen, and no matter what I'll stand on the fact that this baby will be born.

It's eight o'clock, and I'm nervous. Tori and I get up around seven and order breakfast. I'm amazed at the fact that the food is still being held down.

"Are you going to call him?" Tori asks.

"I can't."

"Yes, you can. Do it."

"Okay, but he's going to be pissed."

"Who gives a fuck?"

I start dialing the numbers. My hand trembles from the thought of Jalen's tone of voice. I hear the line pick up.

"Hello," he answers in a calming voice. Thank God. Maybe he's slept off some of the anger.

"Jalen, it's me—Kaye. We need to talk."

"Alright. Where are you?"

"On my way, coming back to you."

"Okay. I'll be here when you get here."

I hang up, concentrating mostly on composing myself. Maybe he'll be okay now that he has had time to think.

Tori drops me off, and I thank her. I take the green mile walk to the door. I ring the bell, and Jalen opens the door immediately.

He glares at me. I know at that moment he's pissed. He picks up the Tiffany vase resting on the console table and slams it against the wall. Oh, my God, please don't let him kill me. This can't be happening again.

"Who in the fuck do you think you're dealing with, Kaye? I ain't no small, piss-ant niggah around the block. You sneak out of my muthafuckin' house in the middle of the night. Do you think I'm gonna put up with that shit, huh?"

"Jalen, I—"

"Jalen my ass, bitch. You will not fuck up everything I worked for and just the thought…The thought of me actually wanting to be with you. Thinking that you were different. How could I be so stupid?"

"Jalen, it's not like that. I'm not like that. I'll take care of the baby. You won't have to do anything. I promise. I've never asked you for anything, not even this," I say, pointing to my belly.

He walks away with his hands cupping his forehead. "Okay. Okay. Do you love me, Kaye?"

"Yes."

"Do you wanna be with me?"

"Yes."

"Good. That's all I need to know." He turns around and walks toward me. I become at ease. Finally, he understands. But before I can dwell in that peace, he yells at me from the bellow of his soul, "Get in the damned car right now, or I'll end it for the both of you, right now."

My world has just shattered into a million pieces. Jalen has just threatened my life and the life of my unborn child. I don't know if he actually means it, but the look in his eyes verifies it.

When he finally stops yelling, I start walking to the truck, sobbing the whole way, dumbfounded and confused. He's acting as if I've set him up. I could call Tori. She'll come and get me, but he must read my mind.

"Don't even think about calling Tori. This is between you and me, and let's keep it that way."

We drive the entire route in silence. I have no idea where we're going, and I'm too afraid to ask. My eyes are so swollen, I can't read the signs. He's blaring rap music, and now I have a headache in addition to heartache.

We finally pull into a small clinic. It's not like the ones you see on TV where the people carrying signs are outside screaming and shouting. He parks the car and gets out. He walks over to my door, opens it, and escorts me out. He's going to make sure that I go through with this. There's no way out.

The clinic is actually nice inside, but scary nonetheless. Jalen goes to the desk and pulls out a stack of bills and places it in the receptionist's hand. I curl up in a chair and begin to rock back and forth uncontrollably. The tears begin to pour, and I feel like a little girl who has no one to play with. I'll never forgive Jalen for this.

I feel him hovering over me. I turn away so that he isn't able to touch me. I hear my name. It's the nurse. I don't know why she's calling me by name. I'm the only one in the waiting room. I can't move. My legs don't work anymore. I look up to see her helping me up, escorting me to the back while handing me a gown.

I put on the gown and sit on the table, shaking.

"Relax, precious," the elderly woman says.

I can't reply. I'm scared.

"It's okay. I'm just going to do an ultrasound. This jelly will feel cold but only for a while," she tells me while simultaneously pulling up my gown.

I turn to look at the monitor, and I see it. My baby. Helpless. Defenseless. I start shaking again.

"Oh, precious, what's going on?"

I look at her through puffy eyes, "I don't know...I don't want to do this."

"Then why are you here?"

"Because he's making me."

"This is your body," she states firmly. "You should have never let anyone, especially a man, brow beat you into this. If you don't want to do it, then don't. No matter what he says. There are women every day who go at this alone and do a damned good job. Do what's best for you."

"He's not going to be supportive."

"Oh see, that's the beauty of this thing. You don't have to beg him to do anything. There are two choices for him. He can do it either by choice or by force. He was responsible enough to get down with the act. He needs to be responsible enough to deal with the consequences."

She prints out the ultrasound and hands me the pictures. "This is something you helped to create. Baby, a lesson learned is a lesson earned. Learn from this. View it is a mistake, but have the faith to know it will work out in the end for your good."

"He threatened me though."

"Then you press charges. Stay away from him. Is he outside now?"

"Yes. He's just...I don't know. He's so different from when I met him. He says he wants to be with me, but..."

"How can he say he wants to be with you and deny you when you're about to give him the best of you?" she insists, pointing to the sonogram.

"I don't know. I don't know what to do anymore. He's going to be furious."

"He'll get over it."

"Thanks for not judging me. Thank you for comforting me. I guess it's time to face the music."

I walk slowly toward the waiting area, holding the sonogram tightly, preparing myself for the worst. Jalen's on the phone. I wonder who he's conversing with. My head begins to feel boggled. Excuses float around. Which one can I use? Before I can gather my thoughts, he spots me.

He nods.

I look away. The nurse comes out and gives me a hug. At that very moment, I felt uplifted. I feel stronger. I turn to Jalen. He walks outside. I follow.

When I get in the car, Jalen looks at me and shakes his head. "Why are you doing this, Kaye?"

"What are you talking about? What am I doing?"

"You thought I wasn't going to find out. The secretary told me you didn't go though with it."

"How many times have you been to this clinic, Jalen?"

"Enough."

That confirms it. I mean nothing to him. "Jalen," I say barely above a whisper, "I'm not trying to hurt you. I'm not after your money.

I'm trying to do the right thing. Why won't you see that?"

"I've seen it too many times already. My teammates are mentally fucked up because they're in court every time they're not at a game...every time they negotiate a new contract. I'm not trying to go through that."

"I'm not trying to put you through that. All I'm

asking is that you see it through your unborn child's eyes."

"Don't do that."

"Do what?'

"Make the baby have a voice."

"But the baby does have a voice, and it's my obligation to make sure that voice is heard."

"I don't want this," he murmurs as he shakes his head.

"What did I mean to you?"

"Why are you asking me that?"

"Just answer the question, Jalen."

"It ain't about you, Kaye. I promise if you keep this baby, whatever we had, whatever we could have had is over."

"How can you be so cruel?"

"I'm not being cruel, just careful."

And with that smug retort, we ride in silence the rest of the way back.

When I wake up from my stress-induced sleep, we are at Jalen's house. I wonder what he's up to. He opens the door and I freeze from panic, I realize I can't trust him anymore.

"It's okay. I know what you're thinking. I'm sorry. I should have never went off on you like that. I just need you to see that a baby...it's not the right time." He walks away with his hands gripping the back of his head. "We just met."

"I know, Jalen. It can work. All we have to do is put forth some energy."

"No, Kaye. No. No. No. If you want this, fine. I'm not going to beg you to do the right thing. I have a season to worry about. My plans don't include a baby. You want this, do it on your own."

After his tirade, I find myself not able to cry anymore. Okay he's made his point. I'm on my own. I reach in my purse and dial Tori's number.

"Kaye, are you okay?" she immediately asks.

"I'm fine, Tori, but can you come and get me. I'm at Jalen's."

"Sure, I'll be there soon. Kaye—"

I interrupt her because I know what she's about to ask. "I'm still pregnant."

I hear a sigh on the other end. I disconnect the call and lay back, resting my head on the headrest. I stare up at the horizon. I realize that tomorrow will bring a whole new world.

Tori is making tea for me. I'm holding Coco forcefully, realizing that soon the feel of her furry coat will be replaced by soft, tender, precious skin. I smile at the thought.

"Here you go." Tori awakens me from my dream.

"Thanks."

"It will make you feel all better, and it will help you sleep. You're going to need all the sleep you can get once the baby is born."

"How would you know? You have a nanny."

"Very funny, Miss Thang. I'm glad to see you smiling though. What's up, girl?"

"I don't know, Tori. I don't know what I expected from Jalen. He told me that if I go through with this, there's no chance for us. He says he wants to be with me, but he doesn't want our baby. That doesn't make sense to me. How could he want me and reject our child?"

"Men have been doing this since the beginning of time, yet women have stayed strong. You'll be fine. And besides, I'll be here to help you through it—or at least Sarella will," Tori said, referring to her nanny.

"Yeah. Thanks, Tori, but I'm going to have to do this on my own. I never thought I would be raising a child by myself. I can't believe he left me hanging. He threatened to kill us both."

"No way."

"Yes way. After he threw a vase against the wall. He apologized later, but it didn't mean anything to me. How could he, Tori? How could he treat me like a groupie? I never pursued him that way. I never asked him for anything. I just wanted to be happy and be friends. He escalated things."

"I think that Jalen is just not paternal. He likes to party. He's not trying to be tied down. But by all means, make his black ass pay child support."

"That's just it. He said he didn't want me leeching off him and messing up his game plan. I swear if I didn't know for myself, he really thinks I'm a trick."

"He's just being a man."

"No. He's just being a fucking asshole, but if that's the way he wants it, that's the way he's going to get it. I bet you never had to worry about Dre."

"No. When I met him, he was family oriented. Jalen didn't grow up with his father."

"That's what I don't understand. Knowing how hard it was for him, why would he want his child to endure the same fate?"

"I'll get Dre to talk to him, you know to see where his head is at."

"Up his ass," I say in absolute disgust.

"Maybe he just needs some time to get adjusted to the change."

"Yeah. Right."

"Well, get some rest. I'll call you tomorrow. I know this is easier said than done, but don't worry. Things always have a way of working themselves out."

"That's what everybody keeps insisting."

I awaken to the sun shining through my bedroom window, now realizing its significance. I've made it to another day. I scoot out of the bed, almost knocking Coco to the floor.

"Sorry."

She only growls in dissapproval.

Today I have to do the inevitable. I have to make a lot of hard decisions. The first being to get a doctor's appointment since lately all my visits have been via the emergency room.

Next, I go online to view my savings to see how long I can live at my current status. I will not allow Jalen to use money as a way of getting me to do what he wants. I'll make it on my own without him. This baby will be just fine, although I may have to miss a few meals.

The ringing phone startles me, and I realize, it must be Tori.

"Hello."

"Hey, Kaye. It's me—Jalen."

"Yeah."

"How are you doing?"

"I'm fine. What do you want?" I say, short tempered.

"Kaye, I need you to understand where I'm coming from. I enjoy spending time with you, and maybe sometime in the future, we could—"

"Stop it, Jalen. I've had enough of your torture and badgering. When we made...had sex we were two consenting adults. You knew that there was a possibility that this could happen, especially since we weren't using protection, so I won't take the brunt of this. We created a child together."

"I know, but it's just not a good time right now."

"When will it be a good time? When you're married to someone else? When I'm fifty? When you're retired, or better yet when I'm dead? I realize now that you had no intention of being with me ever. But that's okay. I'll be okay. My baby will be fine. He or she will grow to be big and strong. So, it's you, Jalen, who's going to wish you would've made a better decision. Not me. To end this once and for all, I don't want you. I don't want your money. I definitely don't wont your altrusive ways imposed on my child. Yeah, I may struggle, but that's okay. Unlike you, I'll do anything for my child. So here it is. Don't call me anymore. You have nothing to offer me now. I have the best of you growing inside me," I say and hang up.

Whoa, that felt really good. "Okay, Coco, let's start our day."

I fix me some toast and juice and pray that it will stay down.

I head to the shower. Standing under the nozzle feels really good. The water hits my body at all the right spots. It is relaxing and rejuvenating.

After I get dressed and head to the front door, I jump in fright.

"Oh my goodness, Tori, you scared the shit out of me. You could've let me know that you were here. You know the baby doesn't respond well to stress."

"No, the baby doesn't respond well to drama. Two totally different things. I'm sorry. I just wanted to make sure you were okay."

"Thanks. That means so much to me right now. Jalen called this morning, trying to get me to reconsider."

"I can't believe him, Kaye. I'm so sorry that I hooked you up with him."

"You didn't exactly hook us up—although you did initiate it, you didn't hook us up. That was all on us."

"I know, but it just doesn't seem fair."

"Yeah. Life isn't fair. I guess you just have to roll with the punches. It's not just about me anymore. It's about this little guy," I say as I rub my stomach.

Ooh, Baby, Baby

I can't believe I'm seven months already. It seems as if time has flown by. Thank God for Tori. I've been stretching my money because I still don't have a job because the doctor thinks it's best that I don't work. Tori's been buying a lot of stuff for the baby. I think she still feels a little guilty about what happened between me and Jalen. I don't blame her—it's not her fault. Jalen is a grown man. He should stand up and own up to his responsibilities. I haven't talked to him, although Dre occasionally gives me messages from him that aren't the least bit helpful. I'm learning to depend on me. As a matter of fact, I've been doing it for a while now.

Today, Tori is going with me to the OB-GYN. I am excited because I get to find out the sex of the baby. No matter how tough times get, I know I made the right decision.

All of a sudden the phone rings, redirecting my thoughts.

"Hello."

"Hey, girl. It's Tori."

"I know."

"Then why isn't your fat ass down here?"

"Tori, I'm not fat. I'm pregnant."

"Same difference. Hurry up before the baby heads out and takes it's own self to the doctor."

"Why must you always be so dramatic?"

"Watch your mouth, heifer, and move that fat ass."

It's not even worth arguing. I hang up the phone and gather my things. I know Tori loves me, but sometimes I don't think she likes me very much.

As I approach the car, I smile instantly as I see my goddaughter waving at me from her car seat. I hop in and start talking to her. And naturally, Tori goes into her drama mode.

"Well, hello to you, too, bitch."

"Excuse me. I just got off the phone with you, remember?"

"Whatever. I hope your baby weighs eleven pounds."

"Now, Tori, that was just cruel."

She looks at me and gives me a sneaky smile. "So, what do you think you're having?"

"I don't know."

"Well, being the professional that I am—"

"What makes you a professional?"

"Hello, do you not recognize the masterpiece in the backseat?"

"Yes, I do, and what a wonderful work of art she is. But that doesn't qualify you as a professional seeing how you only have one."

She rolls her eyes and continues, "As I was saying, I think you're having a girl."

"No kidding. It was hard for me to tell with all of the pink attire that I've acquired. On the contrary though, I think that I'm having a boy."

"Oh, yeah. I hope he looks pretty in pink."

"Bitch."

"I'll remember that."

As we get out to head into the doctor's office, Tori grabs her Louis Vuitton bag, and I grab Nyla's hand, and she and I walk together.

"Seriously though, Kaye, I think you're going to be a wonderful mother."

"I hope so."

Sitting in the waiting room for what seems like an hour, the nurse finally calls my name. I'm so excited that I almost trip. Tori looks at me and shakes her head in disgust. I just roll my eyes and head toward the exam room with Nyla in tow.

"Good morning, Kaye."

"Good morning, Dr. Robertson."

"How are we coming along?"

"Fine," I reply as I sit Nyla next to Tori. I sit on the examination table, ready for the results. The gel feels cold on my stomach. I wince. For some reason, I can't get adjusted to that feeling.

The doctor points to the sonogram, and oh my goodness, the baby is sucking its thumb. How cute. I look at Tori, and she's full of smiles.

"Okay, Kaye, let's see if we can determine the sex of the baby. Move your leg, sweetness," the doctor commands.

I move my leg, hoping it will encourage the baby, and nothing happens.

"Maybe if I move around, the baby will too." So with that notion in my mind, I get up and do a little jig and wait for the baby to make a move. Finally, the legs come open, and I be damned.

"Ha! I told you I was having a boy. I know my body," I say to Tori smugly.

"Since when? Whatever."

"Yes, it is a boy, and he's handsome. Have you thought of a name for him yet?" the doctor asks.

"No, I haven't," I reply.

"I know one name he won't have for sure," Tori retorts.

I look at her sternly, and she bursts out laughing.

"Well you still have time. Everything seems to be on schedule. I'll see you in two weeks, okay?" the doctor says.

"Great," I say, still reeling from my little victory over Tori.

As we're pulling out of the hospital parking lot, Tori asks me what I would like to do for the rest of the day.

I look at her and reply, "Go shopping, but first let's go back to my apartment."

"For what?"

"So we can take all that pink stuff back." I begin to laugh hysterically.

"Uh-huh, keep it up. Just keep it up."

We both laugh, and even Nyla joins in.

We have an exhausting mall trip, exchanging all the pink items for blue ones. It never ceases to amaze me how Tori can spend hours upon hours in the mall. Dre keeps calling like he thinks we might have been abducted. Tori tries to convince him to meet us for dinner at the Mexican restaurant in the galleria. From the look on her face, I can tell he's with Jalen, but that's cool. Jalen will live to see the day that he will regret everything that he's done to me.

I'm so relieved when we finally make it home. My feet are killing me, and my back feels as if it is on fire. I thank Tori for everything and rush inside my apartment.

I dash to the bathroom and draw me a warm bath with chamomile and jasmine. It is definitely time for us to relax. The baby has become relatively active, and I think he's tired.

The bath has a sort of rainy-day effect on my body. I'm so relaxed. It's like my mind and my body are on a different journey. It's my mind that is wondering aimlessly.

I can't help but think back to times when Jalen con- fessed his so— called feelings for me. How could I let myself fall so deeply? Who am I kidding? I don't want to raise a baby by myself. It will be too hard. I'm not ready. Maybe Jalen was right. It's too late now. I just have to suck it up and press on.

It's Sunday, and it's service time. I try to make it a point to visit the house of the Lord. I grew up in the church. My grandmother made sure, regardless of the fact that both my parents were deceased, that I stayed in the will of God. To this day, even after my grand- mother's death, I'm still in church. Thank God for Grandma because I surely don't know what I would do without the Lord.

Tori and Dre are supposed to be picking me up for the eleven o'clock service. Pastor Williams is one of the most dynamic preachers I know as well as an awe- some orator. He delivers the type of sermons that just make you wanna wave your hand, and the choir sings songs that make you wanna step out in the aisle. That's why I love New Hope Baptist. It makes me feel like I'm in the country at the little wooden church by the railroad tracks.

It's ten o'clock, and I need to eat something and get dressed before Tori and Dre pull up at ten-thirty. I grab a burgundy sweater and a long blue jean skirt. By the time I grab my Bible, Tori is walking in the door.

"Good morning, sinner."

I look around to see who she's talking to.

"Don't get crass with me, tramp. You know exactly who I'm talking to."

"Why are you calling me a sinner and a tramp, Tori?"

"Well considering your current predicament…"

"Tori, that's not funny."

"Oh, lighten up. It was just some Sunday morning humor."

"I don't find that funny."

"Well neither does the church, but let's go."

As we pull up to New Hope, the parking lot is full. When we enter the foyer, we are greeted by the ushers who hand us programs and tithing envelopes. We find our seats in the middle of the church and wait patiently for service to begin. Nyla comes and sits on my lap.

I look around the church to get a view of my surroundings. This is a technique I've used for years, usually as a precaution just in case something jumps off and I have to make a quick run. I see elderly ladies dressed in white with hats so big they make the rest of their bodies disappear. Just when I'm about to redirect my focus to the front, a silhouette catches my eye. Of all the days Mr. Wonderful decides to come to service at eleven o'clock or at all for the matter, why did it have to be today? He is not going to crush my spirit. I rebuke that demon in the name of Jesus.

I must have been staring too long because Tori turns around to see what I'm looking at, and unfortunately so does Dre. He motions for Jalen to come sit with us. I look at Tori and roll my eyes seven hundred and twenty degrees. *Lord, just hold my tongue please,* I begin to pray.

When he sits down, I turn my head in the opposite direction.

"Good morning, saints," he replies.

Now I know good and well that didn't come out of his mouth.

"And sinners," Tori retorts. Dre gives her an evil stare that I know she'll have to account for when she gets home.

"Hey, Nyla," Jalen croons.

Her response is to flee from my lap right into his arms. Traitor. It's amazing how he could be so affectionate to someone else's child and do all he can to deliberately hurt his own. Lord, just give me strength.

Thank you, Jesus, 'cause at that moment the choir begins to sing. Everyone is thoroughly enjoying the musical selections as expressed by the "amens," "hallelujahs," and "sing y'alls." Tori even stands up and starts clapping and rocking to the choir's rendition of "War Cry" by Micah Stampley.

By the time Pastor gets up to preach, the church is already on fire. Pastor Williams looks around the congregation as he approaches the podium. "Good morning, church."

"Good morning," the church responds in unison.

The pastor reads the topic scripture from the Bible and begins his sermon, "This Too Shall Pass." He preaches about learning to stand and go through trials. He tells us that we may lose the battle, but we're guaranteed to win the war. He's indeed a great orator. I look at the mother's bench and all the mothers are passed out, caught in the spirit. Ushers are running around the church with fans and smelling salt, trying to revive those slain in the spirit.

I look to my left, and Jalen is sitting like he's at a funeral. Go figure. He looks directly into my eyes and then at my belly and back to my face. Nothing. Tori sees this and shakes her head.

By the time all the saints have been gathered, hats and wigs returned to their rightful owners, and the sin-sick have their repentance at the altar, we are at the benediction.

Walking out the door, I can see the pastor in the foyer shaking hands and kissing babies. He shakes Jalen's hand and congratulates him on a wonderful season, all the while looking at me from the corner of his eye.

"Sister Kaye, Sister Tori, Brother Dre, did you enjoy the service?" he asks

"Yes," we all respond.

I try to grab Nyla's hand, but evidently she is stricken by Jalen's handsomeness because she runs straight into his arms.

It will be a chilly day in hell before I buy her any-thing again, little traitor. She is grabbing his nose and he is cuddling her. Lord, please forgive me, but I hope he burns in hell.

Jalen walks over to us holding Nyla's hand, and he and Dre start discussing lunch plans. They've decided to go to Chili's. There is no way I'm going along on this little party. Dre is going to have to take me home. I turn around to tell Tori, and I'm interrupted by the pastor.

"Sister Kaye, may I have a word with you in my office?"

Hmm. Now that's strange. The pastor has never asked to see me in his office. We usually meet in the conference room. He closes the door behind me and gestures for me to take a seat.

"Kaye, I've been informed of your situation."

"What situation?" I inquire.

"Your pregnancy."

"Oh, you couldn't tell by looking?"

"That's not what I'm referring to."

"Then what exactly are you referring to?"

"Jalen."

"What about him?"

"He informs me that he may be the father of your child."

"He is the father of my child," I say boldly.

"He seems to think that he was mislead."

"Mislead?"

"Yes. He thought you appeared to be someone different. He thinks that after you lost your job you set him up so that you could get pregnant."

"He told you that?" I scream in rage.

"Yes, Kaye. I understand. I'm not saying I agree with him. You're a hardworking young lady with a good head on your shoulders. You're above this. You know that you can come to the church for anything."

I stand up in fury. "How dare you? Who in the hell do you think you are and better yet who in the hell does Jalen think he is? I've never asked him for a dime. I told him that he was about to be a father. When did you all decide to have a round-table discussion about me, casting me as a wayward hooker and gold digger?"

"Kaye, that's not what I mean."

"Yeah, I know exactly what you mean. I've been coming to this church for years. Just because Jalen decides to drop a couple of hundred thousand your way doesn't mean he's the blessed one. He's irresponsible and a liar. I didn't pursue him, and of all the people in the world, I would hope you would know better, but I see I'm sadly mistaken. The fact that Jalen would even question the paternity of this child sickens me. Since you and him are in cahoots and have become the best of friends, the both of you can rot in hell together."

"Now, Kaye, calm down. There's no need to speak like that. Everything is going to work out fine. After the paternity test, I'm sure you and Jalen will be able to come to some understanding. Right now, you need to just view this situation from his eyes. Athletes get set up all the time."

"No, Pastor, the only eyes that I need to view this situation from are those of my baby. So you can tell your buddy I said fuck him, and every dog has his day and his is surely coming."

And with that, I slam the door and walk out of his office. Just like that, betrayed by a monetary donation. I don't need this. As I am rounding the corridor to join Tori, I hear Pastor Williams call my name. On the brink of tears, I ignore him. I look up. I can see confusion in Tori's eyes. I don't want to explain. I just want out of here.

Tori grabs me and stops my progression out of the door. "Girl, what's going on?"

All I can do is shake my head. The next thing I know, I feel Judas's hand on me.

"Kaye sweetheart—," I spin around and shoot him a look that death itself will not approach— "it's okay. I didn't mean to upset you."

"What's going on here?" Tori continues to ask.

"I resign from every board I sit on and withdraw my membership," is all I can muster before the floodgates open. Tears are everywhere.

"Kaye, you don't mean that," pleads Pastor Williams.

"Oh, I mean it, and I put everything I love on it."

"Kaye, don't speak to Pastor like that," Tori begs.

"What's wrong?" When she receives no answer from me, she looks to Pastor Williams who just waves her away. Luckily, everyone has already left and doesn't get to see this little Oscar-worthy performance.

I continue to walk out the door, ignoring Tori's and the pastor's pleas. All of a sudden, I don't feel so good. By the time I reach the exit, my head is spinning like I'm on a roller coaster. The last thing I hear before I hit the floor is Tori shouting, "Somebody call an ambulance."

It Hurts Like Hell

I come to in the emergency room. There's a scurry of doctors and nurses in the room. I am scanning the room for Tori. I see her against the wall crying. It finally hits me, I passed out. I feel my stomach. The baby is still there. I feel the nurse stick an IV in my arm. I am in excruciating pain.

"Miss Parker, I'm Dr. Mark Thomas. We have to perform an emergency C-section on you. It's best for the baby." I nod to let him know I understand.

"Prep her for the Cesarean," I hear the doctor say to the elderly nurse, but as they are prepping me, the pain gets more intense and suddenly the sheet is wet.

"Her water just broke," the nurse yells.

I start to panic. "What's going on? Somebody please help me."

The nurse begins to rub my shoulder. "Miss Parker, please try and relax."

"Relax? What are you talking about? Oh my God. This hurts like hell," I scream in agony. "Please don't let my baby die."

Tori runs to my side and tries to calm me down, but I can't. The force is just too strong.

"It's coming. I have to push."

"We're getting you ready for a Cesarean," the nurse informs me once again.

"Well, hurry up," I grunt through my teeth.

Tori keeps trying to feed me ice chips. Although it is helping me some, I am still sweating like a pig. Finally, I can't help it any more, I have to push.

The doctor comes back in. "Kaye, I want you to listen to me." I shake my head. "When I say push, you do just that, okay."

Before I can agree, I'm pushing.

"I didn't tell you to push yet," the doctor states.

"I'm not doing it by choice," I yell angrily.

After what seems like forever, I finally hear a scream and then the acknowledgement that it's a boy.

"Whew, never doing that again," I say in exasperation. After the nurse weighs him and stabilizes him, she takes him straight to the neonatal intensive care unit, allowing me a glance at him on the way out. I cry. Not so much because I'm happy but because I'm terrified. Will he be okay? He's two months early.

I look at Tori, and she just holds my hand and whispers, "He'll be fine."

"Okay," I say not quite sure that I believe it. As I am just about to settle down, I have a sudden urge to push again, so I do.

"This is just the afterbirth," Tori says. The nurse comes over and looks at the monitor. "Oh my God, it's another one."

"Another what?" I scream.

"Baby."

"No, no, no, not happening again," I scream in between grunts. The doctor rushes back to me. Just like that, a repeat performance. I feel like I won't make it through this. I am crying and pushing at the same time. I am extremely exhausted. When I finally have the last push, the doctor announces that it is a girl. The nurse weighs her and rushes her off to the NICU, only allowing me a sneak peek.

I am exhausted, scared, in pain and tears, all at the same time. Tori is desperately trying to reassure me.

"It's going to be okay. Trust me. I'm going to call Dre. Try and get some rest. You'll need all your energy to take care of those precious babies."

Everything seems as if it is in a haze. My body begins to drift into a place of serenity. The nurses' voices begin to fade. I can no longer hold on to consciousness. I turn my head to the side and silently pray that my babies will be okay.

As Jalen opens the door, Kaye is resting. The room is too quiet. She looks so peaceful sleeping. He doesn't want to wake her, but as soon as he moves, she begins to stir.

"Tori?" she asks groggily.

"No, it's me Jalen," he says as he pulls a chair next

to her bed.

"My babies. I need to see my babies," she murmurs as she tries to sit up.

"Umm, I think you should just lie down right now."

"I can't. They're mine. Since you don't care about them, somebody has to."

"Kaye, it's not like that. I love being with you. Kids, they change everything."

"How can you say you love me, Jalen, when you hung me out to dry? You told Pastor Williams that I chased you down and trapped you. You lied to protect your name and character while you drug mine through the mud."

"It wasn't like that, Kaye."

"Oh yes, it was, Jalen. I never tried to hurt you. I tried to take things slow. You act as if I knocked you over the head and took your sperm."

"Kaye—"

"No. No matter how you feel about me, don't neglect your children. They deserve better."

"Kaye, I told you I'm not ready to be a father. I can't do it. Things would have been great between us had you just went ahead and got the abortion. Maybe later on when we've had enough time to get to know each other we could have started a family. It's too soon."

"Whether it's sooner or later, it doesn't matter. They're here. That's all that matters. Even if you don't step up and be a man, I still have to be a mother. Jalen, I'm begging you, don't do this. Don't walk away from them. They need you."

"Kaye, I can't." Jalen sighed. "We've been over this a hundred times. You knew how I felt, but you went and did what you wanted to anyway."

"It's call being responsible."

"I need to get my mind right."

"You know what, Jalen? You've made your decision. I'm through begging and pleading. It's obvious you're not going to change, so I'll do it for you. I love my babies. Since the moment I found out I was pregnant, I decided I would live for them. There are kids who grow up every day without fathers. There are mothers who step up to the plate and make things happen, so I'll make it easy for you. From this moment on, I exonerate you from paternity—financial, emotional, and social responsibility from me and the twins. Stay away from me and stay away from them. We'll be fine without you. Now get the fuck out."

After Jalen opens the door, the nurse walks in with a wheelchair. "Kaye, it's time to visit the twins. Are you coming, too, sir?" she asks Jalen. He looks at her and walks away.

It takes everything in me to try to keep from crying. It's pointless. I let the tears stream from my eyes. Not just out of hurt for me but out of the not knowing what the future holds for me and my kids.

As the nurse helps me in the wheelchair, she asks, "Are you alright, Miss Parker?"

I looked at her and smile. "Yes. I just need to see my precious babies."

Part Two

Living and Learning

It Ain't My Fault

Three Years Later . .

It's been pretty rough parenting on my own. The twins were really sick when they were born. They had jaundice, respiratory distress, and respiratory syncytial virus, known as RSV. They were on ventilators for two months. When we finally thought they were doing better they became anemic. I was in and out of the hospital for half the year. I was tired and pissed. I was going through hell. Even my dog, Coco, got sick and died, while Jalen was living his life without worry.

Money was tight. I had to go to work. I heard about this position in Houston doing research for a hospital, and I took it. I couldn't depend on Tori forever. I left and I got my life together. It was hard, but Tori, being the friend she is, always came whenever I needed her, and I'm so thankful for that.

I've been back in Atlanta for six months working for a small research firm. I had to come back. I was missing home terribly and most of all I was missing Tori. The twins are doing so much better. They are very energetic, and they love playing with Nyla. I think Nyla enjoys their company more than she let's on.

Dre has also been great with the twins. Whenever we come to his home, he treats the kids as if they are his own, and they love him dearly. I'm so glad to have friends who care.

Today is a beautiful Saturday. Tori and I are supposed to be taking the kids out to the park and maybe the zoo. They'll have such a great time.

"Cami and Cam?" I say to my twins, Camille and Cambden.

"Yes, Mommy."

"Are you guys ready? Put away your toys. Aunt Tori will be here soon. I'll just tidy up the kitchen a bit."

As soon as I grab the dish towel, the phone rings. "Hello."

"Hey, Kaye. It's me Dre."

"Hey, Dre. What's up?"

"I was wondering if you wanted to bring the twins over. We're going to barbecue outside and watch movies later. We could make a day of it."

"Where's Tori?"

"She's here."

"May I speak with her?"

"Sure."

"Hey, heifer," she says as soon as she answers.

"Hey, Tori. What's going on?"

"Dre has decided he wants to have a barbecue and

fun day. I don't know who in the hell he thinks is going to prepare the shit. He gave Simmy the day off. He's barking up the wrong tree."

I fall out laughing. Dre is always trying to domesticate Tori. Not happening.

"I don't know why you're laughing. You better get your ass over here now or else you'll be raising Nyla because I swear if he keeps barking off orders, I'ma cut his ass."

"Okay. Calm down. I'm on my way. Do you need me to bring anything?"

"No. Just that lovely smile and your unbridled passion for cooking."

"Bye, Tori." I hang up and tell the twins let's go. I know Tori, and she means everything she says.

Tori is waiting outside for me with her arms folded and patting her foot, when I pull up. It doesn't take us that long to get there, so I don't know what her problem is.

I get the twins out, and they run and hug their aunt Ri Ri as they affectionately call her.

"Why are you standing outside?" I ask, bewildered.

"Because it's a barbecue. Cam and Cami, go play with Nyla in the backyard. You and me, let's go the kitchen." I follow her without question.

I look around, and the kitchen is in total chaos. "Tori, what happened?"

"Absolutely nothing."

"I see that. I start preparing the potato salad and the macaroni and cheese. Tori, how many people are coming to the barbecue?"

"Well, it's just us…and…"

"And who?" I ask.

"Kaye, look, it wasn't my idea."

"What wasn't your idea?"

"Dre thinks that somehow you really wouldn't mind if Jalen came to the barbecue because you're my friend and Jalen is his friend and—"

"Heartless. That's what that sick bastard is. He thinks he can waltz his no-good ass in here and everything will be all good. The hell with him. Thanks for inviting us, but we have to be out. Cami and Cam, time to go."

"Wait, Kaye."

I turn around on my heels. There is nothing that she can possibly say to make me change my mind. "Why?"

"Because you deserve to go where you want without having to worry about who you're going to run into. "Stop letting that loser dictate how you live your life. At some point, at some time, the twins are going to ask questions about their father. Just make sure your end is covered. I don't want him here either. I'm just tired of answering questions from him and Dre. Go ahead and get it over with. Besides, my babies are playing, and I will not allow anyone to interrupt that."

The twins enter the kitchen looking despondent

and almost at the brink of tears. "Mommy's sorry," I say. "We're not going home. Go back and play. I'm going to help Aunt RiRi fix lunch. Are you guys hungry?"

"Yes, ma'am," they reply in unison.

That still trips me out how they can finish each other's sentences and answer questions simultaneously. When they were babies they didn't fall asleep at the same time. Go figure.

Tori and I—or rather I—did a great job with the food. Everything looked wonderful. Dre had the meat smelling so good, I forgot just how hungry I was until my nose encountered the aroma. We headed outside to meet Dre.

"Yo, Kaye, I love you like my sister. Jay's my boy. I love him like my brother. I love the twins like they're my children. When you kept them from him, you kept then from me. The only reason I even told Jalen about the barbecue is because he's always asking questions about the twins. You guys refuse to talk to each other. You're always being so secretive. I've been feeling like I'm walking on eggshells with you all. I'm sick of it. I love you all, but there will be peace in my house today. There will be understanding and forgiveness. You have about fifteen minutes before Jalen arrives. That's enough time for you to gather your composure. We have lots of closets in this house. Choose one."

Tori and I both stare at Dre with our mouths open. He's never vented at me before. I don't think Tori's seen this side of him either. She looks just as shocked as I do. Speechless, I look at Tori and shrug. I mouth the words, *I'll be fine.* I head upstairs to Tori and Dre's room. If I have to deal with Jalen today, I'm choosing Tori's closet. It's the size of a bedroom.

It takes me all of fifteen minutes just to talk myself into going back downstairs. At some point, I'm going to have to face the demon—literally. Dre's right. Damn. Damn. Damn. Why me? Let me get my ass out of this closet before R. Kelly writes another episode starring me.

I walk downstairs. It seems as if it is taking me forever to get there. Suddenly, Tori appears in front of me. "He's here."

"Great," I say sarcastically, clapping.

She rolls her eyes and walks outside. I follow her. Jalen and Dre are in the driveway talking. Conspiracy. Nyla, Cam, and Cami are playing on the slide.

"Cam, stop," I yell. He plays entirely too rough with the girls. He's pulling the girls off the slide as they each slide down and dragging them. What surprises me is the fact they actually let him do it. I'll have to have a talk with him about the treatment of girls.

Nyla looks around and spots Dre talking with Jalen. "Uncle Jay," she yells and rushes with her hands outstretched. The twins, never to be left out, run straight to the prodigal father.

"Cami, Cam," I scream, "back here now." They stop, turn around, and come to me. I grab each one and place them on either side of me. I can see Jalen staring at me while hugging and picking up Nyla.

"Kaye, don't be so mean," Tori says as she undoubtedly sees the hurt in the twins' eyes.

"I'm not being mean to him. I haven't said one word to him," I say to her in self-defense.

"Not him. The twins," Tori says as she looks from Jalen to Cam and Cami.

I look down, and they're both staring at me all glossy eyed.

"Mommy's sorry," I say and give them a big hug.

"Let's get lunch ready for the kids," Tori says. I take the twins and sit them down at the picnic table. Nyla comes over to me and taps me on my knee.

"Yes, sweetie."

"Auntie Kaye, you forgot to give Uncle Jay a hug."

I turn around and he's directly behind me, so I guess I can't say what I'm thinking.

"I'll give him one later," I reply. "Sit down. What do you want to eat, guys?"

"I want a hot dog." That would be Cam.

"I want barbecue." That would be Cami. She's just like her mama, a straight sucker for a pig.

"I want barbecue chicken with none of that messy stuff. I don't want it on my clothes." That would be Nyla, a true princess' daughter.

"Okay. Everybody let's eat," Dre says.

Tori sits to my right—symbolism. I look around the table. Every seat is full except the one to my left, and Jalen sits his ass down like we're all chummy. I won't say anything. At least he's not sitting by my children.

"Mommy, cut my meat for me please," Cami says.

"I'll do it," Cam yells.

"Cam, if you pick up that knife, you're going to be in big trouble."

Today is definitely not the day for him to be showing his tail. I cut Cami's meat up so she can use her plastic fork to pick it up. All of a sudden, I've lost my appetite.

"What's your name?" Cam asks Jalen.

"My name is Jalen. What's yours?"

"My name is Cambden but you can call me Cam."

"Hi, Cam. It's nice to meet you," Jalen says as he extends his hand to Cambden.

That little gesture does it. Now I feel as if I'm about to hurl. I roll my eyes at Cam in disappointment. I specifically told him to never talk to strangers. He's cut from the same cloth as his father.

Tori notices this. I can tell because she elbows me in the side. "Hurry up, you guys," she tell the kids. "We can watch movies after you eat."

"Aunt RiRi, can we watch *Madcar?*" Cami asks. Everyone starts laughing. She gets offended and pokes out her lips.

"Cami sweetie," I say, "it's *Mad-a-gas-car.*"

"Oh," she says and repeats after me. "*Mad-a-gas-car.*"

"Very good," I praise.

She stares at Jalen. She doesn't ask any questions. She just stares. I watch their little display. He smiles at her. Nyla gets a little jealous and rushes over and jumps in Jalen's lap.

I'm cutting her completely off.

"Uncle Jay, let's go play," Nyla says.

"Okay, sweetheart, but Uncle Jay has to talk to Auntie Kaye first."

I drop my fork in shock. I really can't believe this bastard thinks I'm about to have any kind of conversation with him.

Dre feels the tension and tells Tori to escort the children into the theater room. "But I want to stay," Tori says, pouting.

"Tori, please go," he begs. She gathers the kids and rushes them off into the house.

I know good and well Dre and Jalen don't think I'm about to let them gang up on me. If so they have completely lost their minds. I look at Dre who is looking under eyed at Jalen.

"Oh, to hell with this," I say as I jump up and head to the house.

"Kaye," I hear Jalen call, but I never miss a step.

"Girl, what did you talk about so quick?" Tori asks.

"Shit. Because I have nothing to say to that black bastard."

"Ooh, Auntie Kaye you said a bad word," says Nyla all giddylike.

I turn around and scold her, "Little girl stay out of grown folks' business."

She begins to pout just like her mother. "Sorry, Auntie Kaye."

Now I feel bad. I've never lashed out at Nyla before. She must be devastated. "Auntie Kaye will watch her mouth, okay?" I say to soften the wound.

She just nods.

"Don't be coming up in here taking your frustrations out on my child," Tori chides.

"Sorry. I think Dre and Jalen were trying to gang up on me."

"How would you know? You didn't stick around long enough to find out."

"Whatever," I say as I sit down and watch *"Mad Car"* because that's what I feel like at the moment.

Is it just me, or are cartoons getting more grown up? We laugh so hard, I almost forget about my situation completely until I get up to take Cami to the bathroom and Jalen's standing in the doorway.

"Kaye, we need to talk."

"Fresh out," I respond.

"It will only take a minute."

"I don't have a minute. Can't you see I'm taking *my* daughter to the bathroom."

"Don't do that?"

"Do what?"

"Personalize them. They're mine too."

"Since when? When did you have that epiphany?

Or better yet, who pointed that out to you, Dre? It's amazing how twisted you are."

"Mommy," Cami cries.

"Hush, Cami. Mommy's talking."

"Don't do her like that. She can talk if she wants to."

"Since when did you ever care about her talking? As far as I can remember, you walked out on her before she could barely breathe, so don't stand there all self-righteous. You don't know what's best for my children."

We must be pretty loud because Dre and Tori both come to see what is going on.

"Kaye, grab a hold of yourself," Tori shouts.

"He started it," I whine like the kids, pointing to Jalen.

"Started what?" Jalen asks, looking all stupid.

I feel nudging at my hand. I forgot Cami was standing there. I look down. She's in tears because she just used the bathroom on herself.

Dre is fuming.

"You two are pathetic. The one chance you get to make this situation work out for the twins, you ruin it."

By this time Cami is bawling.

"Come with Auntie RiRi. I'll get you dry," Tori says to Cami to encourage her.

And with that, my daughter rushes away with my best friend. I turn around to see what the other kids are doing. And of course, they're standing up in the seats looking at the whole little altercation.

"Jalen, didn't I tell you to use some tact?" Dre says strongly.

"I was just standing here watching them. She got up. I wanted to talk. She was the one doing all the screaming, not me."

"Like you didn't provoke me," I fight back.

"You know what, forget it. You two can be so twisted. I only invited both of you here at the same time…" He stops and looks at the little faces peering over the recliners. "Nyla and Cam, go play upstairs."

They rush right past us.

"I thought you two were mature enough to handle this situation. Oh, but was I wrong. It's not going to work, and the sad thing about it is the people you hurt are the very same people you both pretend to love so much. Jalen, you are dismissed." Then he turns to me and shakes his head.

Jalen leaves out the door. I feel elated. I don't have to deal with him anymore.

"Thanks, Dre," I say all happy.

He spins around on his Nikes. "No, ma'am. you aren't getting off that easy. You know better."

"What?"

"You know better, Kaye. Everybody makes mistakes. When they come to you asking you for forgiveness, what are you supposed to do?"

"Huh?"

"What are you supposed to do?" he yells.

"Damn, you don't have to treat me like this," I say behind eyes full of tears. "How could you be so mean to me after all he's done? I knew you would take his side."

"If your brother spites you, Kaye, what are you supposed to do?"

"You can't be serious."

"Oh, but beloved, I am. If your brother spites you, what are you supposed to do?"

"Why do I always have to be a Christian?"

"What are you supposed to do?" he demands.

"Forgive him," I yell at the top of my lungs.

"See, that wasn't so bad. It took an act of Congress to get you to sign the bill, but doesn't that make you feel better?"

"No," I say through gritted teeth.

"Oh, really? Kaye, you are dismissed."

"Whatever," I say as I head upstairs to get my babies.

"Where are you going?" Dre asks.

"To get the twins and take them home."

"As godfather to those precious kids, I am enforcing the rights that you granted me. You are in no condition at this present time to make rational decisions for the twins. Hence, you are dismissed until further notice."

"You must be out of your mind if you think that I would leave my kids here so that you can give Jalen free reign over them."

"Point proven. It's not about you. It's not about Jalen. It's about the twins. It's supposed to be all about the twins. You've let your anger override any possibility they might be happy. Has it ever occurred to you that just maybe the twins might want to get to know Jalen? Did you ever ask them? No. You didn't because you were too busy trying to hurt Jalen because he hurt you. You see, you don't have your children's best interest at heart. I'm declaring you temporarily unfit."

"What?"

"You heard me. I will not let you reduce those kids to pawns. I love you, Kaye. Now get out."

"Who died and made you boss?"

"You. You forgot about the kind and caring person you used to be."

I can't believe I'm leaving without my kids. I'm mad as hell, but short of calling the cops, I know there's nothing I can do. Dre is livid. I walk to the door bawling, tears expelling from my gut. My body is trembling uncontrollably. I could kill Jalen for doing this—making things worse. The twins and I were doing so well.

"Kaye," I hear Dre call, "if you see my friend, tell her I miss her and I love her, and I need her to be the strong, caring person she used to be. The world already has enough evil people in it. I don't want her to turn into one of them."

I lower my head in shame and bolt like lightning out the door.

Truth Hurts

I t's been two weeks since Jalen showed up, I embarrassed myself in front of the kids, and Dre called me an "unfit" mother. Tori brought the twins back yesterday. I was so happy to see them that I actually cried. Tori told me that Dre told her what happened. She said she agreed with him, and I just need some time to myself but I wasn't an unfit mother and he had no right to say that to me. I felt so relieved. I was starting to believe it.

The twins have awakened from their nap, and now they're being tiny terrors, running through the house tearing up things. I don't have the courage to discipline them because of all the things they had to endure at the barbecue, so I let them have their way.

The doorbell rings, and I answer it.

"Miss Parker?" a courier asks.

"Yes," I reply.

"You've just been served."

"Served?"

"Good-bye, ma'am," he utters as he walks away.

I open the papers, and it's a petition for visitation rights for the twins. Damn Jalen. He just won't leave it alone. I do the only thing I know to do—I call Tori.

"Tori, he did it. I can't believe his smug ass. After all this time, he thinks he can just walk back in here and everything will be okay. Sadly mistaken. I won't stand for this. If he wants to play hardball, so be it. I'll master this game and show him how it's done," I say before hanging up.

I hide in the bathroom drowning myself in my own tears for what seems like hours. Tori bursts through the door. "What the hell is wrong with your crazy ass?"

I hand her the papers, shaking them in her face.

"Girl, I thought something had really happened," she says, reading through the papers.

"Something did happen. He's trying to take my children away from me."

"Get a grip. It's a petition for visitation rights, not a custody battle. Let the man see his children for goodness' sake, Kaye."

"But...I need a lawyer. He's going to pay out the ass. We're not married, but when I get through taking him to the cleaners, he'll think we were."

"You need Jesus. Are you losing your mind?" Tori says as she tosses the papers to the side.

"Why does something have to be wrong with me? He's the one who left."

"Yes, but he's back, and he wants to make amends,

so let him."

"He went to the courts."

"You wouldn't compromise, so now you're letting someone else make that decision for you."

"It's not fair."

"Kaye, I don't know what to say. You do need a lawyer to help you come to a reasonable agreement."

It's been three weeks since I received that petition. I still don't feel like I've had enough time to get prepared for this day.

Walking into the courtroom makes me nervous, Tori and Dre both come. I don't know whose side Dre will take, but I definitely don't think it will be mine.

Tori holds my hand as my lawyer, Eric Battle, walks up to me. I'm nervous as hell. I don't know what to expect.

"Miss Parker," he states, "remember this is just a petition of visitation rights. Before any of that can happen, paternity must be proven. When the test is done and confirmed, we will file a petition with the court seeking child support, which will work out in your favor tremendously seeing how he hasn't contributed time or finances. The judge will not take that lightly."

"So, how can I stop it?"

"Stop what, ma'am?"

"I don't want him to see the twins at all."

"There's nothing you can do about that now but let

nature take its course," he says as the bailiff walks in.

"All rise. The honorable Judge Lancet presiding," the bailiff says.

We all stand on cue, and sit when we're told.

"We have a petition for visitation rights, is that right?" the judge asks.

"That's correct, your honor," Jalen's lawyer chimes.

"Has paternity been established?"

"No, your honor, a paternity test has not been done. At your request, we would like to have one performed this afternoon," Jalen's lawyer asks.

"Motion granted. We will reschedule two weeks from this date upon confirmation of said paternity test to establish visitation rights. Court adjourned."

"What?" I say to my lawyer.

"Everything is fine," he tries to reassure me. I wasn't buying it. "Everything's on schedule."

I look over, and Jalen's staring at me blankly. I roll my eyes and walk away. Son of a bitch. Every dog has its day, and his is soon to come.

The twins have no idea why we are at the hospital. They're looking around like they've never seen one before. As much time as they've spent in one, they should be very familiar with the scene.

My lawyer waves, and I walk over to him. "Are you ready?" he asks.

"I don't know. I think the twins are going to freak out."

"No need to worry. The nurses here are great. Jalen has already been in, and he's gone, so that's one factor out of the way."

The nurse calls the twins' names, and I walk them into the exam room. It's cold in here, and Cami is about to cry.

"Mommy, I'm not sick," Cami whines.

"I know, sweetie, but the nice nurse wants to put a big Q-tip in you and your brother's mouth. It will be over in a minute."

"No," Cam says. "No."

"It's okay," the nurse says as she asks Cam to open his mouth and swabs it. He looks at me and looks at her then looks at Cami who says, "Cam's a big boy." Cami seeing how easy this is quickly allows the nurse to do the same to her.

It's been two weeks since the paternity test. The results, of course, are conclusive. My lawyer has already requested child support. If I can't keep Jalen from seeing the twins, I will make him pay out the ass. I'm seeking ten thousand a month plus back support of five hundred thousand. See how he likes that.

The courthouse is somber, reflecting my emotions. It's hard to believe that there could be a chance today where Jalen will get to see the kids. If I could keep him away from them, I would forgo the money. My lawyer walks into the building and greets me.

We walk into the courtroom, and Jalen and his

lawyer are already seated. I quickly turn my head and take my seat.

"All rise. The honorable Judge Lancet presiding." We stand on cue.

"In the matter of Kaylondria Parker versus Jalen Matthews, are both parties present?"

"Yes, your honor," both the lawyers say in unison.

"Miss Parker, I understand you are seeking financial support for your twins, Camille and Cambden Parker, who are fathered by Jalen Matthews. Is that correct?"

"Yes, your honor," I say.

"Explain yourself in regards to the amount sought.

"Your honor, I am seeking ten thousand dollars a month and five hundred thousand dollars back support. Mr. Matthews, as I'm sure you know, is a wealthy NFL player who has shunned his parental duties for three years. In this time, he has not given me a dime and has made no effort to contact me. I lost my job and was forced to live hand to mouth for a whole year while my children who were born premature fought for their lives. Mr. Matthews was well aware of the situation, and he walked out. Now, he wants to return and play daddy. I'm not having it."

"Is this true, Mr. Matthews?"

"Well, your honor, not entirely. Miss Parker and I had decided when I found out she was pregnant that we would not keep the baby. She went behind my back and decided to keep the baby."

"Mr. Matthews, this is irrelevant. Your responsibility is to your children. You have sat out of the dance for too long. Every child needs the love and support of a father."

"Your honor, that's why I'm here. I want to have a vital in part of my children's lives. I know I haven't done my part, and it was wrong to leave when she needed me the most. I know I can't get back the years and all the moments I've already lost, but I can start now. I want them to get a chance to know me and me to know them. I'm different. I'm changed."

"Mr. Matthews, that is admirable. I understand you are also seeking visitation rights."

"Yes, your honor."

"Well, after looking at all the paperwork on file from Miss Parker, I order you to pay fifteen thousand dollars a month in child support and back support in the amount of eight hundred thousand dollars. This will help cover medical expenses and child care as well as court fees."

I smile with delight.

"Mr. Matthews, I also grant you weekend visitation. With the first visit, the mother will be present. This will help the transition. You are dismissed. Court adjourned."

I am furious. Jalen can come in and do whatever the hell he wants. He gives a sad speech, and everybody falls for it. One of these days, Jalen's going to have to pay for the error of his ways.

I walk out. My lawyer approaches the bench. I can't breathe. The walls are closing in on me. My lawyer approaches me outside the courtroom and informs me the first visitation is scheduled for this weekend. We have to choose a mutual place to take the kids. You know what I say? "You're completely worthless. My life is going to completely change after this."

When I pick up the twins from Tori's, she's standing outside. I get out of my Sequoia.

"Hey, girl, how are you?" she asks.

"I'm fine, just pissed. How are the twins doing?"

"Dre has them upstairs playing video games with Nyla. What happened in court?"

"Jalen gets to see the kids every weekend."

"That's not bad, Kaye."

"How can you say that?"

"Kaye, it's not. How much money are you going to get?"

"It's not about the money. I don't want him around my children."

"So how much?"

I look at her and roll my eyes. "I got fifteen a month and eight hundred back support."

"Thousand?"

"Yes, Tori."

"That's good. You can do a lot with that money, like pay off hospital bills.

"Whatever. Why does everyone take his side?"

"It's not taking his side. It's doing what's best for the twins. They deserve to know who their father is. Don't deny them. It will all work out in the end. You'll see."

"Yeah, I bet," I reply.

I've been dreading this day since I found out it was going to happen. Jalen's first visit. I'm really not in the mood, and if he pisses me off, I'll end it before he realizes it. I've decided that we should meet at the park and then go to Kids World, a big game room for kids. They love that place.

I haven't told them yet about Jalen because I'm not quite sure I know how. As I pull into the park, I spot the prodigal father sitting by the slides.

"Mommy, are we going to play?" Cambden asks.

"Yes," I reply. "There's somebody you're going to meet today."

"Is he a stranger?" Cami asks.

"Well, not quite. You remember the man at Aunt RiRi's?"

"Yeah," Cam replies.

"Well, he's meeting us here."

"Okay," Cami replies.

I let the twins out to go meet Jalen. He spots us and starts walking toward us. I immediately halt. I don't know what I was thinking. I'm totally not ready for this.

"Hi, Kaye."

"Whatever, Jalen," I respond.

"Kaye, let's not do that today." He looks at the twins and rubs Cam's head.

"He's not a puppy, Jalen."

"He looks just like me."

"And you needed a blood test to confirm it."

"Hey, guys," Jalen says to the kids, ignoring me.

"Hi," they reply in unison.

"My mommy doesn't like you," Cami says. She's so attentive.

"It's not that she doesn't like me. It's just she's a little mad at me right now."

"Oh," she says understandingly.

Why does he always do that, make everyone see things his way.

"My name is Cam. That's my sister Cami. We're twins."

"Well that's good," Jalen says. "You guys are so smart."

"We're three."

"How about we go sit down at one of the tables?" Jalen asks.

"I wanna slide," Cami disapproves, whining.

"It will be only for a little while. Me and your mother want to talk to you guys."

I roll my eyes so hard they almost pop out of their sockets.

We all sit down at the table like one big dysfunctional family. Jalen looks at me for reassurance. Fuck him. He's on his own.

"I guess you're wondering why we had to come here, huh?"

Cami raises her hand like she's in class.

He looks at Cami and smiles. "You're too cute. What is it?"

"I know."

"You know what?"

"Why we're here?"

"Okay, so tell me."

"Are you my daddy?" Cam interjects before Cami has a chance to answer. She turns around and punches him in the face.

"Cami, why did you do that?" I ask furiously.

"'Cause I was going to say the answer," she replies, pouting.

"That's still no reason to hit your brother." I reach for her and swat her hands twice and now she's crying.

Jalen looks at me disapprovingly. "Yes, Cam, you're right. I am your father, and I love you both very much."

I wonder where they got that piece of information from. They're just like sponges.

"We love you too," Cam says.

What? After everything I've been through, how does he keep getting things to go his way.

"Well, can I have a hug?"

They both jump up and give him the biggest hug I've ever seen. They don't even hug me like that.

Figures. You do all you can for kids, and they still don't appreciate it. I get up, kick the table, and go back to my car. Since they love me him so much, let's see how they like staying with him. I drive off and watch them in the rearview mirror, and they don't glance back.

I drive to Tori's in fury. I walk in the door, and she's sitting in the den.

I burst into tears as soon as she says hello.

"Girl, what's wrong?"

"They love him already. They're playing with him at the park right now. I was livid. He sat there with the biggest smirk on his face. I hope he dies."

"Kaye! Stop it. How could you say that? Don't do that. Why do you continuously torment yourself?"

"I'm not. I don't have to. Jalen's doing a damn good job on his own."

"The football season is about to start again. Let the man see his children. Let them get to know their father."

"Why?"

"Because it's the right thing to do."

"They're not even loyal to me."

"Girl, they're children. They're loyal to everyone. Besides, the holidays are approaching. They're finally going to have a real Christmas."

"So, all the Christmases with me weren't real?"

"That's not what I meant, and you know it.'"

"I'm going home." I leave out, slamming the door

and never looking back.

Soon as I get home, I turn on the bath and add shea butter bath oil. I soak away the day's woes. I start sobbing. I feel like Jalen is interfering with my life. It's funny how he wants to do now what I begged him to do three years ago. It could've been so much better. He doesn't have the right to interrupt my life now.

I wake up twenty minutes later. It's amazing how a bath can be so relaxing.

I put on some sweats, make me some tea, and turn on the TV. Great, a Lifetime movie is on. I watch the movie in its entirety.

By now it's six o'clock. I'm missing the twins. I grab my keys and start heading for the door. When I open it, Jalen and the kids are standing outside. The twins run right past me and head upstairs. I then shut the door in Jalen's face. We have absolutely nothing to talk about.

Today's Sunday. It's two weeks before Thanksgiving. Time has been flying by. The twins have been loving every second they've been spending with Jalen. His mom, Delores, has been spoiling them to death. Every time they come back from visiting her, I always have to spank them. They even had the audacity to tell Jalen I spanked them. He tried to question me about it, but I bet the hell he'll never do that again. The money has really helped a lot and Jalen's always on time with his payments. I decide that the twins and I are going to spend Thanksgiving with Tori, Dre, and Nyla. Tori and I are going to cook—against her wishes, of course. Dre is still trying to domesticate her. It might be working. She actually washed clothes the day before—with my assistance of course.

It's Thanksgiving Eve, and I'm on my way to prepare the food. The twins are excited. They think it's Christmas.

I pick up my ringing phone, look at the caller ID and push the button on the side. I am not negotiating plans for Thanksgiving with Jalen. He can forget it.

To my surprise, Tori has peeled potatoes and put all the items I need on the counter. I am so proud of her.

"You go, girl," I say.

"What up, Kaye?" Dre says as he comes into the kitchen and scoops up the twins. "We're going to the movies. It'll give you ladies a chance to cook without interruption."

"Thanks," I mumble. My relationship with Dre is still a little strained ever since the incident at the barbecue, but we try to be cordial to each other. He is still my children's godfather.

"Girl, I'm so glad he's gone. He was getting on my last nerve," Tori says.

"Oh, really?"

"So you go ahead and do your thing. I'm going to

watch TV in the theater room," Tori says.

"No, you're not. You're going to stay your ass in here with me and help me cook. You can turn on the TV in here. Besides, I need someone to talk to."

"Okay, but I ain't cooking shit."

"That's fine."

"How are things with Jalen?"

"The same. He just called. I didn't answer. He's always trying to make plans with the twins. It pisses me off."

"I think it's great. You better get used to it. It's for life. He's finally doing what you wanted him to do. Leave him alone."

"Why does everybody always take his side?"

"Nobody's taking sides. We just want what's best for the twins," Tori says as the phone rings.

She answers and hands it to me. "It's for you." I roll my eyes because I already know who's at the other end.

"What?" I say, irritated. I turn my back to keep from having to see Tori's stare.

"Hello, Kaye. Why do you always have to be so rude to me?" Jalen asks as if he doesn't already know.

"You don't know?" I question.

"Look, I don't want to argue. I was wondering if–"

"No," I say before he goes any further.

"But you didn't even give me a chance to finish what I was saying."

"It doesn't matter. The answer will still be no."

"Kaye, I know I hurt you, but this is ridiculous.

Everybody else has forgiven me, except you."

"Well, Mr. Wonderful, you didn't leave everybody else with two small, sickly children."

"Why is it so hard for you? The twins are thriving. They're loving the fact that they have two parents who love them."

"One didn't leave them out to dry."

"Kaye, for the thousandth time, I'm sorry. I'm not the same man I used to be. I just want to do right by the twins. Why won't you allow me? We can't even be in the same room together. That's not healthy for them."

"Oh, so now you're concerned about their health? Fuck you, Jalen," I say and hang the phone up before he can utter another lie.

"I'm sick and tired of his smug ass, Tori."

"Girl, relax. You're going to have a nervous breakdown. It's not even necessary to be so angry. Let go and let God."

"Whatever," I say as I start on the Thanksgiving feast.

I go downstairs to heat up the food I prepared the night before. I didn't finish cooking until eleven o'clock.

I prepared chicken and cornbread dressing, turkey, macaroni and cheese, green beans, ham, sweet potato pies, peach cobbler, lemon pound cake, mustard greens, corn, and potato salad. All I need to do is butter the rolls and pop them in the oven. The twins are still sleeping, so I head upstairs to wake them and get them and Nyla dressed. On my way to the bathroom, I can hear the sounds of Tori and Dre's lovemaking. They make me sick.

I manage to get everything ready, including the children, by eleven- thirty. Tori finally decides to grace us with her presence and help me set the table.

"Girl, you've outdone yourself. I can't wait to eat."

"Where's Dre?"

"Taking a shower," she says as she looks at me and winks.

"Slut."

"Jealous bitch," she replies.

I am just about to curse her out, but the doorbell rings, and she goes to answer it. I get the kids seated, and just as I am about to head back into the kitchen, I hear something that makes me quiver.

"Daddy, Daddy," Cami and Cam say, running to Jalen. I turn around so fast I think I give myself a concussion.

"What the hell are you doing here?" I ask.

"Kaye, don't start. I was invited."

"By whom?"

"Me," Dre answers. "Kaye, please, let's be cordial. Today is Thanksgiving. We're going to be thankful, okay?"

I roll my eyes and go sit down at the table with my arms folded. I watch Jalen carry the twins and place them in their seats.

"Now that everybody's here, let's say grace. Jalen, do you want to do the honors?" Dre asks.

"I would love to. Everybody, bow your heads please."

I look around, and everybody's head is bowed except for mine. Jalen looks at me like he's waiting for me to oblige. He can wait till the cows come home because it's not going to happen. When he finally realizes this, he begins with his prayer.

"Dear Lord, we come here today to thank you for all the wonderful blessings you have given us. We thank you for the massive feast that has been prepared before us. Lord, we—I mean, I—want to also thank you for a second chance…a second chance to make things right, not just for me but for my precious children. Amen."

"Amen," Tori and Dre reply.

"Bravo," I cheer. "You have an incredible gift for words. Have you ever thought about running for political office? You sure do have the qualities."

"Kaye," Tori shouts, "not in front of the children."

"Don't start, Kaye. I'm sick of your little mad black woman routine. We were having a perfectly good time until you decided to ruin it. I won't continue to allow you to put my children through this," Jalen lectures.

"Your children? Your children! Where the hell were you when your children were on ventilation machines fighting for their lives? Where in the hell were you when your children had to be rushed back and forth to the hospital? Where in the hell were you all the nights I stayed up praying that God would help them get better. And now, you have the audacity to sit here and thank him for your children."

"I'm not perfect, Kaye."

"You're damn right."

"I've made mistakes. I'm trying to own them and move on. You can't see past your own hurt to allow our children a future with me. What's so bad about that? I'm not letting you ruin this for everybody else. How many times can I apologize for the same mistake, huh? I have the children for this weekend. I have papers from the court. If you wanna break bad, we can. I'm not leaving. If you can't stand to be around me, then you leave. It's my first Thanksgiving with my kids, and no matter how far I've fallen, I still have the right to be redeemed, and thank God that redemption doesn't have to go through you."

"I hate you," I scream with tears going in every direction.

"Kaye, why are doing this?" Dre asks. "Let it go."

"Fuck you, Dre."

"Kaye," Tori shouts.

"Fuck you, too, Tori. You're supposed to be my friend. You knew he was coming, and you didn't tell me. How dare all of you attack me like I'm the one at fault?"

"'That's not what we're doing, Kaye," Tori cries.

"Yes, you are."

"Mommy," Cami cries, "Stop yelling."

I look and Cam has his hands covering his ears with a tear-stained face. Nyla has her head down on the table. I'm mortified. I've just hurt the people who mean so much to me, the ones I've sacrificed so much for.

"Thanks, Jalen, for making me look like the bad guy," I say as I grab my keys and my purse and walk out the door.

"No, Kaye, come back," I hear Tori scream.

Forget it. I'm done. Done with all of them. So much for friendship.

I look outside my window, and it's pouring down raining. So much for a thankful day. I'm alone, and Jalen's happy. I must be doomed to a life of misery. What did I ever do to deserve this? Maybe I should've just let him come back. I'm so hurt. I can't stand to be rejected. I still have feelings for him.

I refuse to stay in this house alone. It's too quiet. The walls are closing in around me.

I grab my keys and my purse. I'll take a drive to get my mind off things. On my way to the door, I also grab an umbrella. A good drive will help me to clear my head, help me get my focus back.

Karma

I've been driving for an hour. I still can't stop thinking about what happened at Tori's. I bet they're just having a wonderful time.

The rain is coming down really hard. I can barely see the road. I need to pull over before somebody hits me or I hit someone else.

I pull over, and I realize that I'm not in the best of neighborhoods. If I would have been more attentive to my driving than my thoughts, I would have realized this. I decide to stay in my SUV until the weather lightens up.

I turn off the engine and turn on the radio. I'm in a pretty secluded spot, so I relax. The rain is so peaceful, I begin to doze off. I try to stay awake, but my body is not putting up any resistance. I give up and go floating into the land of sleep.

I don't know how long I've been asleep, but I awaken to the sound of smashing glass. Oh my God, I wake up to see my front windshield being broken by a brick. There's also a guy breaking my passenger-side window. I try to start the engine, but my window is broken by a fist, and this guy has already opened my door and is dragging me out by my hair.

"Please," I scream, "you can have the truck and my money. Just leave me alone. I have two small children."

"Shut up, bitch," says the guy in the red jacket as he punches me in the face.

I must have passed out because when I awaken, I'm in an old abandoned building. Seems to have been a store of some sort. Thank God somebody rescued me. I get up slowly because I have a pounding headache and my face is swollen and streaked with blood.

As I try to put my feet on the floor, I'm slammed back on the table by the guy in the red jacket. "Please don't hurt me," I protest.

"Yo, fellas, she's awake," I hear him say.

I look up, and three guys appear out of nowhere. They can't be serious. I struggle to break free, but the guy in the red jacket is much stronger, and he rips my shirt. The other guys come to his aid and begin to tear my clothes off me as I scream and plead for my life.

"Shut up," the guy in the red jacket yells again as his fist comes down to my face several times, rendering me semi-conscious.

One by one I feel them having their way with me, violating me over and over. I cry and scream so much that I'm completely hoarse. I pray for death. It has to be easier than to endure this. When I think they are finally finished taking their turns with me, they are only just beginning. They enter me two at a time, violating my body in ways I've never before experienced. The pain is unbearable. I pray again for death. *Why won't he answer me?* I think just before they decide to add the other two to the mix. I fall asleep. "Thank you," I mutter as my mind drifts to another place and my body releases the pain and pressure.

It's been three weeks since I've been in the hospital. I'm doing so much better. I had a seizure and went into a coma, but now I'm coherent and in a regular room. I don't feel much like talking. The doctor says he will release me in three days. I'm told that Dre and Tori already have the house set up for my arrival. They plan to decorate when I get home. They know how much I love Christmas.

I refuse to see the twins because I don't want to scare them. My face is still pretty swollen. Today, Tori said she would bring me magazines and puzzles. I don't talk to her either. It's mainly because I don't know what to say to her.

I hear the door open and it's Tori. The room is filled with the fragrance of fresh flowers. Dre, Jalen, and Tori make sure that the flowers are always fresh.

"Hey, ma. What's going on?" Tori asks me as she brings in a vase of fresh roses,

I don't answer. That's typical. My body is turned so my back is to the door and my face is to the wall. She comes to the wall to sit and talk as always.

"Kaye," she says nervously, "the doctor says he's going to release you in three days. Isn't that great? The twins miss you so much. You'll be able to spend time with them."

I turn to face the door.

"Don't do this, Kaye. I want you to get better. Those sorry sons of bitches will pay for this in the end one way or the other."

I don't respond. That's her cue to leave.

"You know what? I don't care how angry you are at the world or Jalen or how pissed you are at me. I will never stop caring about you, loving you, and doing what's best for you even when you don't realize it. See ya in three days," she says as she walks out the door.

Today, I get out of the hospital. Tori couldn't bear to come get me, so she sends Dre. I've been hearing how wonderful Jalen's been with the kids. Shopping and showing them how to wrap gifts. Although they love him, Dre says they ask for their mom every day. He's said that Jalen has had to rock them to sleep many nights. He informs me that Tori is preparing the house for Christmas. He then leaves to go sign my release forms.

I sigh as the tears roll down my eyes. Today, I have to start my life all over again.

A New Day

D re and I ride home in silence. I already know what awaits: Jalen playing Billy Homemaker. I pretended to be asleep all the times he's come to my room pretending to care. He even had the unmitigated gall to bring the twins in. How could he bring my children to see me like that?

I'm happy to be alive. Everybody keeps telling me how blessed I am. I sure don't feel like it. I'll be glad when Christmas is over. I'm not in the mood, and I don't have anything for the kids.

"Well, home sweet home," Dre says comically.

He can kiss my ass. I haven't forgotten anything. Looking around, I spot Jalen's tricked-out ride complete with car seats in the back. Bastard. I walk slowly to the house behind Dre and enter after him.

Tori is playing Christmas music. I can hear the kids running around playing. I begin to shake. I can't stay here. I have to go. I turn around to leave and I hear…

"Mommy! Auntie Kaye!"

All three of the kids bumrush me, and I can't move. I'm overjoyed and overwhelmed. I hug them so tight.

"Ow, Mommy," Cambden screams.

"I'm sorry, baby," I say.

"We missed you, Auntie Kaye," Nyla says. "Are you all better?"

"Yes," I lie.

"Mommy, Mommy, it's Christmas," Cami shouts excitedly.

"I know," I say, holding back tears.

I look up, and Tori is smiling. I turn my head so she won't witness the tears. My body begins to heave from stress and pain. I feel as if I'm about to pass out. She notices, and apparently so does Dre because he makes it to me before she does and carries me into the living room where Jalen is sitting among immaculately wrapped gifts.

He looks at me and fixes his mouth to say something, but after seeing my expression, he soon changes his mind.

"Okay, girl, since you're home and feeling better, we're getting ready for Christmas."

I look at Tori like she's lost her mind. "You guys go ahead. I don't feel up to it." I stand and walk away very slowly and head upstairs to lie down.

I hear a knock at the door a few minutes later. I turn to see Jalen stepping in.

"What do you want?" I snap.

"I just wanted to see how you were doing."

"I'm fine."

"Kaye, the twins are so excited that you're home. They've been missing you so much. We promised them that you would help them decorate the house for Christmas."

"I don't want to."

"Why?"

"I don't feel like it."

"Kaye, I'm sorry about what happened to you. Don't punish the kids. They've been looking forward to this. You didn't want to see them in the hospital, and that crushed them. We told them that you were still feeling bad and you needed some time to get well."

I wipe away tears. "I don't want them to think I don't love them and don't have time for them."

"Then come down and show them. It's not about me. It's not about those motherfuckers who violated you. As their mother, you have to be sure that they'll be okay, not saying that you don't have a right to be hurt because you do. They still deserve to have a good Christmas. It's our job as their parents to ensure them that."

"I'll be down in a second, okay?" I say to Jalen. I know he's right. I know he loves them and wants the best for them. I'm just still too hurt, physically and emotionally.

A few minutes later, I walk downstairs and watch

as the kids are decorating the tree, looking like little elves. I feel so empty. They've grown so much it seems in the past few weeks.

"Are you okay?" Tori asks.

"Yeah," I say unconvincingly.

"I baked cookies," she tells me.

"Stay away from them," Dre demands.

"Dre! The twins like them. So does Nyla."

The twins turn around with their mouths full of cookies.

I take a seat on the chaise and start stringing popcorn. We do this for hours, and by the time we finish, the house looks like a winter wonderland. Tori helps me bathe and put the twins to bed. I didn't realize how much I loved bathtime. The kids are having so much fun splashing water on the floor that it actually lifts my spirits.

"Kaye, how are you really doing?" Tori asks.

"I'm just tired, I guess."

"Dre made tea for us. Let's go sit in the great room and talk."

"Okay," I murmur.

We sit in the great room. It's so warm and cozy, the exact opposite of the cold and gloomy hospital.

"Jalen's been great helping with the kids."

"You told me that already."

"Oh," she says, disappointed and hurt.

"I'm sorry, Tori. I didn't mean to snap at you. I just need some time to get used to him being around all the time."

"I know. I just want you to be okay."

"I will. I just need time."

"Take as much time as you need. I know two people who are depending on you."

"I know. Tori, can you keep the twins for me for a little while? I can't do this right now. It's too much."

"I will, but I won't deny Jalen the right to see his children. They need him now more than ever."

"I understand," I say, holding back the tears.

"Kaye, do me a favor while you're at home? Work on you. Don't worry about anything else. Just you."

"I feel like I'm abandoning them."

"You're not. You're going to give them the best thing in this world, a happy and healthy mother."

"Thanks," I say as I walk out the door, leaving my children—again.

It's been a week since I've seen the twins. I've talked to them every day. I actually went out and bought gifts for everyone, including Jalen. I've been seeing a counselor, and she's helped me realize that holding on to the bitterness and anger over the past years is destroying me internally and soon will destroy my life with my kids.

That's why I bought Jalen a gift—actually two, one from the twins and one from me. I refuse to take this pain and hurt with me into the New Year. I had an anxiety attack a couple of days ago. I thought I was going to die. I knew then that I had to let everything go, the hurt by Jalen and the feelings of betrayal by Tori and Dre for supporting Jalen. The rape is going to be different though. I'm going to always have a little reminder of it.

When I went to the hospital a couple of days ago for my anxiety attack, I found out I was pregnant. I didn't even cry. I've cried enough. Those tears haven't changed much. They've just made me weaker, so I've decided to go get my life back. The life I had before the rape, before the twins, before Jalen, and before my ex-boyfriend Derrick.

It isn't easy, but I still try. Each day I go through gives me strength to move on through the next. I haven't told anybody about the pregnancy. Yep, not even Tori. I realize now that I've put her in some unhealthy situations. I need to start doing things on my own. That begins with this baby. I'm keeping it because it has a right to be born. As much hell as I gave Jalen about responsibility, how could I abort it?

I walk into Dre and Tori's house, and it smells so good. Tori's mom and dad greet me at the door with big hugs. Just what I need.

"Hey, girl," Tori shrieks in excitement. "I didn't know if you were coming," she whispers in my ear.

"I wouldn't miss it for the world."

"Let's go unwrap gifts," Tori says as she pulls my arm in the direction of the great room.

"Wait," I say as I hand all the gifts to her father. "I

want to talk to you. I realize now that I've been really stupid."

"No, Kaye—"

"Yes, blaming everybody else for my problems. I had no right to impose on your life drowning you in my sorrows." It wasn't fair to you, Dre, or Nyla, and I'm sorry."

"Oh, Kaye," she says through tears, "don't you know I'll walk through fire for you? Not because you're help-less but because you're my best friend. I know that if the tables were reversed you would do the same thing for me."

"Yeah, I would because I love you."

"I love you, too, girl."

We hug each other for what seems like an eternity.

"Hey, since y'all in the Christmas spirit, Kaye, you better not have come over here empty-handed," Dre says matter-of-factly.

"I didn't," I say, wiping tears. He then hugs me and tells me how much he loves me and how he's prayed for me.

"Thanks," is all I can say. "Tori, can you give us a minute?"

"Sure," she says. "Welcome home."

"Thank you," I say as I watch Tori leave me and Dre alone.

"What's up?" Dre asks, concerned.

"I just wanted to apologize for how I've been acting toward you lately. You've taken a lot of bullshit off me.

I know you weren't taking sides. You were just doing the right thing. I was just so frustrated. I wanted you all to hate Jalen as much as I did, and when you didn't, I felt betrayed."

"We kept telling you we weren't taking sides, but you wasn't hearing it. You let your anger consume you. That's why I took the kids. I wasn't trying to hurt you. I was trying to protect them."

"I see that now," I say as I cock my head to the side as Dre kisses me on my forehead.

"Don't you think for one second if I didn't know that Jalen was legit he would have ever walked back into your life? Believe that. I love you just as much as Tori does."

"Oh, Dre," I say as I hug him, unable to hold back the tears.

"Anyway, I've had a lot of sleepless nights. My gift better be good, or you're going to have to march your little ass out the door and try again."

"Ha, ha," I say heartily. "You're so funny. You should have your own sitcom."

"Hey, great idea. Pitch that to Fox. Let's go into the living room." Everybody is in there, including Jalen and his mom. Dre glances at me sideways.

"I'm straight."

"Good."

I watch the twins unwrap all the gifts. They are so excited. Every time they unwrap one, they go, "Oh Mommy, look, pretty." After the kids exchange gifts, and Nyla thanks me for her Bratz collection, the adults have their turn. Dre gives Tori diamonds. She almost tips over her chair. Jalen gives his mom pictures of him with the twins, and he looks at me nervously. I smile. She cries, saying how she finally can look at them every day. Tori gives me a bunch of self-help books filled with gift certificates. I look at her puzzled.

Her response: "I don't care what anyone says, shopping is therapeutic."

Dre gives me cookbooks with sticky tabs hanging out. I look at him curiously.

"Oh yeah, those are all the recipes I want you to prepare for me, you know, for all the sleepless nights."

"Dre," Tori scolds.

I just fall out laughing. I give Dre and Tori their gifts from me. Dre opens his and sees that it's the new Xbox 360 and starts jumping like a little child.

"All is forgiven," he screams way too excitedly for a grown man.

I shake my head in shame and turn to Tori who already has her gift opened. It's a locket with a picture of me and the twins.

"It's beautiful," she replies.

"You're welcome," I respond.

"Daddy," Cami tells Jalen, "it's your turn. Give Mommy the present."

I look at Jalen, surprised. I didn't expect anything from him. He hands me a card.

Dear Kaye.

I don't really know where to begin, so I'll start all over when I met you. I knew you were different. I loved being with you, and that scared the shit out of me. I was used to leaving in the morning. I couldn't do that with you. When you told me you were pregnant, I punked out. I felt like I was trapped. My father bailed on my mother and then she bailed on me. I was scared that the same thing would happen to us. I wish I would have made a better decision, but I didn't. I just did exactly what I was trying to avoid, running. When you left, I would drive by your apartment. It was then that I realized just how big a mistake I had made. I was trying to hide my feelings for you. I was always telling you that I liked spending time with you, when really I just wanted to be with you but wasn't man enough to own it. I had no right to desert you the way I did. I know you thought I got off easy, but I didn't. My grandmother used to always say that when you make your bed hard, you'll have to lay in it. That's exactly what I did. There were many nights I cried myself to sleep because I was miserable. My career was suffering, and my heart was aching. I prayed to God that if he would give me another chance, I would step up. And so I did. But, in doing that, I forgot about your feelings. I apologize for that. Actually, I apologize for every-thing I've done that's hurt you. I can't take those things back. If I could, it would be already done. I

*just want to make a difference starting now. I
don't know how you're going to take this, but I've
scheduled some counseling sessions with Dr.
Williams. It's funny how we're not married but I
feel like we're going through a divorce. It's okay
though if you don't want to go. I'm still going. I'm
new at this parenting thing and need all the help I
can get. The fact is, Kaye, that I love you and I
want us to be great parents. I want the kids to
grow up knowing what it means to be a good par-
ent, so they won't make the same mistakes we did.
I want them to see us working together and shar-
ing love. I know this will take some time. I'll
wait. I want the best for you and my children.
Love always.*
Jalen

P.S. Open the box please.

I open the small black box and inside is a key.
"What is this?" I ask him.

"I bought you an Escalade. It's outside. Since, you
know...the accident. I wanted you to have something
new to take the kids out."

"Thanks so much, Jalen."

"You're welcome."

I look up, and everybody has tissues. I clear my
throat. "This is for you," I say as I hand the box to
Jalen. He unwraps it and looks at his mom. He then

looks at me, and I give him the warmest smile I can produce.

He pulls out a baby book full of firsts and pictures galore.

He looks at me with tears brimming in his eyes.

"Tori and I scrapbook the kids' lives. I had duplicates made, so everything I have, now so do you." He's speechless. He continues to look at the pictures. He hands his mom the book and sees the DVD.

"This?" he asks.

"The video of their firsts—crawling, talking, walking, you know," I reply.

"Kaye, you didn't...I know—"

"Yes, I did," I respond before he finishes.

"Daddy's happy," Cam says.

"Yeah, you wanna know why?" he asks.

"Why?" Cam asks.

"Because I have twins," he screams as he tickles them, and they fall on the floor complete with Nyla in tow. I smile bittersweetly, now truly understanding a father's role, a father that the child I'm carrying will never know.

"Okay, let's eat everybody. I'm starved," Dre professes.

"You're always starved, Dre," Tori says.

"Yeah, because you never cook."

Christmas turns out to be wonderful. Jalen and I put the kids' toys together. We all sing Christmas carols and take tons of pictures. Who knew making amends would be so therapeutic? I'm finally at that place where I can look at my situation and see the glass as half full as opposed to half empty.

We all go to church for the seven o'clock service. How we manage to make it on time behooves me. Cami coerces her grandmother into picking her up while Jalen carries Cam.

It's been a while since I've been to church, especially this one, New Hope Baptist Church. I remember the last time I was there. I cursed the pastor out. No wonder I've gone through. God don't like ugly.

"Let's find a seat," Tori suggests.

"Go ahead. There's someone I need to see first," I say.

"Okay, but hurry," she suggests.

I take a deep breath and walk down the corridor to Pastor Williams' office. I see him scrambling, trying to get his papers together before service starts.

I knock on the door, and he looks up in total shock.

"Kaylondria Parker."

"Yes sir, it's me," I say as a twiddle my fingers behind my back.

"You look great. Haven't seen you in while. How's life been treating you?"

I look at him and hold my head down.

"Don't you dare. Hold your head up," he says.

"I'm so sorry," I say as the tears impede my words.

"The day you walked out of this office angry and

confused, I was worried about you, especially after watching you being carried away. I've prayed for you every day since then. It's hard to live right when you feel everybody's against you. I realize now that I should have chosen my words more carefully when I spoke to you."

"No. You were right. I messed up too. I wanted everybody to believe everything was Jalen's fault. I carried hatred in my heart for so many years. I had no right to disrespect you, but above all this, I had no right to disrespect God. That's why I've been having such a hard time. I understand now. I just wanted to say I'm sorry and please forgive me."

"You were forgiven the moment you said it," he reassures me with a hug. "You're a good person. You did a lot of things for the church, and everybody misses you. Welcome home, Kaye."

"Thank you. Thank you," I say, exhaling all the way back to my seat.

Service is great, as usual. I see eyes looking at me. For the first time, I don't get defensive. I smile back. The twins are enjoying themselves, clapping and singing to the music. Tori is sitting to my left and Jalen to my right. I'll still have to get used to that one.

Pastor gets up to preach, and we all stand for the reading of the scripture.

"Today, church, I want to talk to you about going from bitter to better."

Everyone instantly looks at me. I shake my head.

He continues, "Sometimes life can place us in situations that we deem unfair. We look around at what everybody else has and think why me. Why must I go through this? Beloved, I'm here to tell you tonight, God leaves no stone unturned. For everything he allows to come into your life, there's a reason. Harboring hatred and going around with a woe-is-me attitude is not how God expects us to handle our situations. His desire is not for us to give hurt for hurt. He wants us to trust and be faithful to know that he can heal any pain, take away any hurt, restore what has been lost, and give exceedingly and abundantly over all things we can ever ask for."

"Preach, Pastor. Tell it like it is," someone in the congregation shouts.

"The only way we can ever reach our goal—the goal that God has placed for us to achieve—is to go through. Even when it hurts, even when we're tired, even when others tell us it hasn't been worth it, let's not hold on to hurt, the pain, the betrayal. Don't take it with you into the New Year. Let go and let God. I'll guarantee he'll show up and show out in our lives. Let's go from bitter to better. Hallelujah."

"Preach! Preach!"

The congregation is on fire. I myself am so touched Jalen has to give me his handkerchief.

Yep. Church is good. Can't believe I stayed away so long. I rededicate my life to Christ that night. I am overwhelmed with how everybody receives me. They are mostly in awe of the twins, giving me money for them. The best thing that happens this whole Christmas is when I go down to the altar for invitation to discipleship, and Jalen comes with the twins. Pastor Williams even blesses them. Maybe everything has worked out for my good in the end. Thank you, Jesus.

It's New Year's Eve, and Dre is throwing the party to end all New Year's Eve parties. I've been eating like a horse. This kid has to be healthy.

"Girl, I'm so excited," Tori screams.

"Why?"

"Because you and Jalen aren't fighting anymore, and now I don't feel trapped in the middle."

"Why aren't you drinking? You love alcohol. Remember you wrote the lyrics for everybody in the club getting tipsy."

"Shut up, slut."

"Tori," I scold her, "don't be so mean."

"You started it anyway, and for your information, I'm pregnant."

"What? Not you, I'm not having anymore kids because I'm popping pills left and right."

"I had been, but I guess it was just time. It happened while I was on the pill. I blame you."

"How?"

"You were stressing me out. My estrogen levels were out of whack."

"Don't be blaming me because you're nasty."

"Whatever," she says.

"Hello, ladies," Jalen proclaims. "It's almost that time."

"Yeah," Dre says, handing Tori apple juice. "No alcohol for you," he says as he rubs her belly. "I want my baby to be healthy and strong."

"Congratulations, you two," I say cheerfully.

"Well, here's to you, baby girl," Jalen says as he pushes Cristal in my face.

"Jalen, you know I don't drink."

"It's New Year's. We've been through a lot. You can have one drink with me to celebrate."

"I can't."

"Why not?"

"I'm in the same predicament as Tori."

Jalen looks at me, Tori spills her apple juice on her clothes, and Dre exclaims, "Oh shit."

"Kaye, how long have you known? What are you going to do?" Tori asks worriedly.

"Chill out," I demand. "I've known since a couple of days before Christmas. I'm keeping it, no matter what. I'll raise it on my own. We'll be okay."

Dre gets excited. "Yes, I'm going to be an uncle again."

"And I'm going to be an auntie," I say as I rub Tori's stomach.

"Me too," she responds by rubbing my belly.

"Oh, so what the hell?" Jalen asks. "I can't be a dad?"

I look at him and respond, "It's okay, Jalen. I can make it on my own. The baby and I will get through this. I won't let what those rapists did to me put a damper on my pregnancy."

He looks at me dumbfounded as he rubs my belly. "I missed the twins growing inside you. I won't miss this one. This baby deserves a father. As far as I'm concerned, you better get used to me being around because I got this daddy thing on lock."

I smile. Who would have thunk it? Mr. Wonderful is actually quite wonderful.

"I'm going to be a daddy," he tells Dre as they each give each other massive bear hugs.

"Girl, we're in trouble," Tori shouts.

"Five, four, three, two ..."

"ONE," we all shout, and Dre holds a mistletoe over me and Jalen's head. Jalen looks directly into my eyes and kisses me passionately. I hear music. Why does this always happen when he touches me? Wait, it sounds different. Sounds like Luther. Is he singing "So Amazing?" Damn right he is.